BOOKS BY MR. CABELL

FROM THE HIDDEN WAY

BEING SEVENTY-FIVE
ADAPTATIONS IN VERSE

BY

JAMES BRANCH CABELL

WILDSIDE PRESS

Published by
Wildside Press, LLC
P.O. Box 301
Holicong, PA 18928-0301 USA
www.wildsidepress.com

Wildside Press Edition: MMIII

TO

BEVERLEY BLAND MUNFORD

(31 May 1910)

"Most blithe and sage and gentle, and most brave!
O true clear heart, so quick to wake and war
Against despondency, lest questioning mar
One hour of living, or foiled hopes enslave
And sour another's living! not to the grave
Do we commit you,—we that, watching, are
As men at twilight noting which bright star
Is leaped at, missed, clutched, swallowed by which wave.

"The star is gone?—So be it. It will rise
Elsewhere, and undiminished. Even thus
We know that instantly in Paradise—
Yea, in the inmost court of Heaven's house,—
A gentleman to God lifts those brave eyes
Which yesterday made life more brave for us."

CONTENTS

MIGONITIS

HORTENSIS

VERTICORDIA

APATURIA

APOLOGIA AUCTORIS

"Vous entendez bien joncherie?"

APOLOGIA AUCTORIS

It is generally known—according to the literary reviewers—that nowadays we are producing an indigenous "new" poetry, of hitherto unknown directness and simplicity; and that, in consequence, America is rendering her poets the unprecedented tribute of purchasing their volumes. Conceivably, at this especial moment, it may be not unsalutary to contrast the output of what Professor Lewis Worthington Smith has well described as "the new naïveté" * with the productions of poets who were in reality naïve. Conceivably, at least, one way of learning what is actually "natural" is to observe the ways of unsophisticated persons. This much preamble comes as warning that hereinafter you may look to encounter, in default of the debatable simplicities of "new" poetry, those genuinely simple melodies which were born of ages less complex.

Poetry having become in some sort a salable commodity, a book of verse no longer absolutely demands, as in the old days, a preface to explain and palliate its existence. None the less, these verses based upon pre-Renaissance formulæ keep to the fashion of their time, and come with a prose pursuivant.

Indeed, the way needs clearing, since the road is clogged with the makings of an ugly syllogism. For

* Compare *The Atlantic Monthly* for April, 1916.

however heartily we admire "the new naïveté," the poverty of thought evinced in mediæval poetry remains notorious; and it is, after all, only the mental gist of a poem which is translatable.

But, in truth, the feature that repels, and troubles us, is not so much that the thoughts of these men were feeble as that their beliefs were firm. The springtide awakens loveliness and human joy therewith, true love ennobles the lover, and death is a terrific adventuring into the dark; such was their simple *credo:* and their belief in its tenets was unquestioning. Now, it is perhaps more subtle to consider spring as a meteorological phenomenon, love as an ingenious device for perpetuating the species, and death as a logical progression toward higher spheres of activity; yet each may be a miracle, for all that; and not to see its wonder any longer may quite conceivably be loss rather than gain. Ophthalmia is at the best an infirm basis whereon to assume airs of superiority.

Just so, these mediæval rhymesters wrote by choice of what to us seems prosaic because to them it was throughout heart-shakingly strange. Their more alert perceptions were aware of a continuous wonderfulness, on every side, which we have learned to overlook. It really is astounding, when you come sanely to think of it, to find a frost-nipped world converted overnight into a place of warmth and beauty; and they said so, in the best language they could muster. We heirs of more sophisticated ages cannot but assent; yet even those few of us who are still guilty of reading a little time-honored verse, say, once in a blue moon, avert with more congenial interest toward the straggling eccentricities of *vers libre* and of polyphonic prose, with such intriguing gambits as "We maidens are many of us older than sheep," and "Hey, old world, shove your staid bonnet over your ear!"

It were flippant to suggest this is the interest that we accord, with livelier concern, to any other approach of the mentally unbalanced. Yet wonder, not bewilderment, is the gateway to the palace of art. The grand power of poetry, in particular, is its interpretative faculty of so dealing with familiar things as to awaken a full and new sense of their strangeness. And life affords nothing more remarkable than its truisms. There is a waggish saying somewhere as to how eagerly we would all scramble for the best seats if God heralded the coming of the crocus by mailing circulars or announced a sunrise via the public journals. The conceit is sound; for Omnipotence would, so to speak, be versifying the commonplace by stressing its importance, much as a noble rhyme and meter emphasize so insistently the thought they clothe that the whole matter dwindles into bathos if (after all) the thought prove mediocre. Yet the real wonderfulness of the terrestrial pageant, even then, would consist, not in its felicities of color, but in its commonplaceness. For the most beautiful and terrible thing about a sunrise is that it happens every day. Just so the sun arose when Pliocene monstrosities held the earth as their heritage, and just so it arose when Christ staggered toward Golgotha; and just so it will arise, every day, when the earth is a frozen clod, trundling voiceless and naked through infinity. A sunrise has nothing to do with man's existence, for all that it serves to time his clocks and rouse his factory-whistles; and therein lies the fundamental beauty of a sunrise, which is above and beyond and indifferent to the utmost reach of human achievement, and is therefore worthy to furnish recreation for human thought.

Here, too, we touch one fallacy of our modernists who insist that poetry should deal with workaday life, and develop the poetic side of shopwindows and streetcars and pessimism. But in shopwindows and streetcars and consistent pessimism is to be contemplated nothing save what man, whether for good or ill, has heaped together in defiance of nature. He made these things, however curious; he knows the elements whereof they are compounded; and he comprehends—there wakens disenchantment—that at a pinch he can patch up something else of pretty much the same sort. Not hereabouts is to be found aught fore-ordained and uncontrollable, or the beauty of fatality—of Ἀνάγκη—and human inefficiency thereunder, such as the old Greeks knew was necessary to art's highest strivings.

And what is this Hellenic Ἀνάγκη, after all, but the commonplace deified, with humanity as pawns? It is assuredly sheer commonplace to point out that more or less unpleasantness inevitably follows an elopement with another man's wife, or that miscegenation tends to shorten life; yet works of very real merit have been based upon these truisms, and nobody worth hearing questions the poetry of the *Iliad* or of *Othello*. Nor is in either case the commonplace an inessential; attempting to imagine Helen as the fiancée of Menelaus, or Othello as a Caucasian, you flounder into the inconceivable.

An element of triteness, in fine, must be conceded as necessary to first class art. That which becomes a classic is, both by etymology and human nature, something which belongs to a class. It is not in any way unique; it is innocent of any "disturbing novelty." Now, neither Ovid's Lynceus or Poe's Dupin, or even the indestructible Mr. Holmes (of Baker Street, W. C.), could plausibly detect any disturbing novelty in the poets of Raynouard's *Choix des poësies originales des Troubadours* and Rochegude's *Parnasse Occitanien:* and when we find these tinkling verses, played always on the two strings of love and death, astonishingly naïve, the thing is partly owing, no doubt, to our superior perception of the proper ends of poetry, but partly too to a more obtuse perception of life's actual wonderfulness. So that in criticism it behooves us, like Agag of old, to tread softly. By the rarest luck, there is no such pressing obligation laid on many of us touching poets—whether immortal or minor—as compels us either to criticize or to read.

A formal bibliography of the sources of this little book was begun, and laid aside as entailing too much labor squandered to no utilitarian end. Petronius and Villon, at worst, require scant introduction to a generation which, the day before yesterday at any rate, was familiar with *Quo Vadis* and *If I Were King.* With Alessandro de Medici, as he misconducts himself in de

Musset's *Lorenzaccio*, many of us preserve a bowing acquaintance, however few extend the intimacy to either his Latin or Italian verses; which, if not positively unknown, would appear to have been overshadowed, even for the specialist, by the similar diversions of his great-grandfather, Lorenzo the Magnificent. Raimbaut de Vaqueiras and his beloved Belhs Cavaliers figure at respectable length in all books treating of Provençal poetry. And Nicolas de Caen has, at any event, afforded the late Mr. Howard Pyle the subject-matter for some striking paintings.

To the other side, apart from any poetical repute, oblivion has swallowed even Antoine Riczi's queer part in the matrimonial affairs of King Henry the Fourth of England. Such unfamiliar names as Charles Garnier and Théodore Passerat and Alphonse Moreau are not likely ever to cut a dash in popular romance; and, for very obvious reasons, just as in the cases of Petronius and Villon, their verses have never been adjudged particularly suitable for undergraduates to worry through in colleges. These, therefore, are indisputably forgotten, if indeed in any general sense they were ever known. Yet here as elsewhere—one would like to think at least, with the discoverer's thrill—the "iniquity of oblivion" has scattered her poppy with rather injudicious cæcity.

If Petronius be not precisely mediæval, he is past doubt more antiquated than his present company in nothing save an accident of birth. And the inclusion of those scattered pieces hereinafter given severally under the name of Paul Verville has seemed on various grounds desirable, in spite of their (comparative) modernity of tone. Into the making of such decisions must always enter, of course, an element of purely personal taste, wherewith proverbially there can be no disputing to the arraigner's profit. To those who do not honor maxims, it can but be answered, with profound irrationality, that all the verses in this book possess at least the common feature of owing their existence in English to the fact that, once upon a time, to put them into English seemed to their transcriber a natural and desirable action. No other bond has ever united the contents of any book of English verse. And although this particular excuse for making rhymes may very often prove inadequate, experience tends to show that any other reason proves so invariably.

In printing a collection of "adapted" verses, there seems to be no Median or Persic makeshift whereby plodding translation may, with the desirable precision, be distinguished from those less faithful paraphrases in which the plagiarist has more temerariously pulled about his larcenies. Upon consideration, this has appeared as satisfactory a rule of thumb as any—to indicate the latter by mention of an author's name, and with the former to include in addition the initial words of the original. The curious may seek out at will the victims of some few unacknowledged borrowings.

DUMBARTON GRANGE
April, 1916.

MIGONITIS

" Pour son amour cut cest essoyne "

I

AT OUTSET

Depart, depart, my book! and live and die
Dependent on the idle fantasy
Of men who cannot view you, quite, as I.

For I am fond, and willingly mistake
My book to be the book I meant to make,
And cannot judge you, for that phantom's sake.

Yet pardon me if I have wrought too ill
In making you, that never spared the will
To shape you perfectly, and lacked the skill.

Ah, had I but the power, my book, then I
Had wrought in you some wizardry so high
That no man but had listened . . .

              They pass by,
And shrug—as we, who know that unto us
It has been granted never to fare thus,
And never to be strong and glorious.

Is it denied me to perpetuate
What so much loving labor did create?—
I hear Oblivion tap upon the gate,
And acquiesce, not all disconsolate.

FOR I HAVE GOT SUCH RECOMPENSE
OF THAT HIGH-HEARTED EXCELLENCE
WHICH THE CONTENTED CRAFTSMAN KNOWS,
ALONE, THAT TO LOVED LABOR GOES,
AND DAILY DOES THE WORK HE CHOSE,
AND COUNTS ALL ELSE IMPERTINENCE!

II

THE OLDEST STORY

"Jadis il était roy d'Argos"
—Antoine Riczi.

He was a king in Argos,
She was a queen in Tyre,
And they went astray from the jogtrot way,
In quest of the heart's desire.

They had pillaged, in royal fashion,
Rare raiments and spiceries
From the marts of Argos, to furnish them cargoes
For traffic in far-off seas;
And before them bright waters parted,
And the wind was fair.

Because
Love leads us—they spoke, light-hearted,—
Who is lord over man-made laws.

The High Gods noted them, idly
Lolling in Paradise,
And remarked they were erring widely
From rules the High Gods devise.

23

But the Most High Gods were wise,
And conceded:—*They are not as We*
Whom no follies beguile; let them go for a while.
Yet presently all men must see
They attain not to where their desire is,
Lest laxity lose Us men's love.
—Thus Wotan ordained, or Osiris,
Or Shiva, or Dagon, or Jove.
—*We must think of Our pontiffs in Argos*
And praiseworthy prebends in Tyre,
Who would suffer dismay did the parish essay
To win to man's heart's desire.

So these two fared ever westward—
Elate, and in love with life—
Amid wide reprehension; for histories mention
These were not husband and wife
Who fared westward, ever westward.
—Beyond the Hesperides,
Where the slow long stroke of their gilt **oars broke**
The lisping of virgin seas,
They viewed the ends of the earth,
Where the Singing Maidens are;
And they still fared ever westward—
Elate, and alone, and afar
From the yelpings of little people,—
For they viewed the ends of the earth.

Then the Gods gave word, and Their thunders stirred
To requite, and to silence mirth;

And that roving vessel was shattered
As a handful of shaken dust
Ere twice it thundered.

All peoples wondered,
And cried:—*Lo, the Gods are just,*
And, look you, abated no tittle
Of punishment due these twain.
Even though They slumbered a little,
We knew They would waken again:
And, whether it was Bubastis,
Or Milcom, or Artemis
Or Baäl, or Zeus, interrupted this cruise,
We knew it would end in this
When he was a king in Argos,
And she was a queen in Tyre,
And they went astray from the jogtrot way,
In quest of the heart's desire.

THE OLD SONOROUS NAMES OF THESE
THAT FARED BEYOND THE HESPERIDES
IN QUEST OF REST AND JOY AND EASE,
LONG SINCE WERE MOCKED AT; AND WERE HISSED
BECAUSE NO GOAL THAT ALL MEN LIST
TO SEEK, THEY SOUGHT,—AND VIEWED, AND MISSED.

BUT LIFE REMAINS LIFE'S PLAGIARIST.

⚜

III

FALSE DAWN IN TROY

"Helenam omnes amunt; invidia semper movente"
—ALESSANDRO DE MEDICI.

THERE is no man but loves her, I well know;
Yet mutinous women, muttering with pinched lips,
Cast side-long glances always when—unvexed—
Queen Helen passes; for she is very fair,
And they have only right and truth with them.

Women remember all the fevered years
This siege has lasted; all its many ills;
The plague; the hunger; the unnumbered men
Who died because this queen is beautiful,—
Men whom they loved, and she loved not at all
Nor even knew by name.

                              None but remembers
How coldly loved lips kissed her in farewell—
Coldly, because for fairer lips than hers,
And for the sake of brighter and tearless eyes,
This man went forth to battle. He thereafter
Beheld the plume of lithe Achilles leap
As flame among the fighting, or beheld

26

The sudden splendor of swart Diomed
Crash through the press of spears; and lay quite still,
Remembering that way Queen Helen has
Of laughter, when the little sigh breaks through
And spoils the music, or her way of speaking,
Which turns to music the most trivial words
Wherein that wonder and that wistfulness
Her voice has always held since Hector died,
Commingles with our rude and alien tongue
As honey with sharp wine. Such idle words
As any man who, with uncovered head,
Waits and makes way when princes will to pass,
May hear of her in passing, gladdened him,
For all that death was fingering his throat
Even now. He was content, remembering her
The Queen.

        For she is very beautiful;
And doubtless Paris, too, gets joy of her
When in that gleaming place which is their home
Her soft arms lift, and clasp his neck, and loose
His helmet—scarcely dented as mine is,
Where that wolf-visaged Greek smote yesterday
Who smites no coward blows to-day, I think.
—But Paris loves not blows. And then he tells
His version of the battle; and they kiss;
And hear shrill women wailing over corpses
Without; and kiss once more. And so he lies
Upon his cushioned couch, and is content,—
Contented just to lie there, still as they

Who fought for his love's sake lie now, and feel
Her fingers moving gently mid his curls,
And hear Queen Helen's laughter.

It is for this
That hollow-eyed Œnone mumbles charms
On twin-peaked Ida; and gaunt Menelaus
Slays silently; and heaven is wroth; and the banks
Of slothful Styx, made populous with them
Whose bodies rot unburied on the plains
That girdle hapless Troy, are resonant
With lamentation.

Thus it is for this
One woman's sake, whose beauty is as a fire
Fed by contending kings with honor and fame
And memories of distant homes and wives,
That all without there is a mighty stir
Of clanging armors, wrangling foreign tongues,
And many Grecian huts about our walls;
And famine and death within. It is for this
One woman's sake—who sleeps now, and in sleep
Smiles, as I think, who may not see her thus,—
That we the common soldiers gather here,
Who are as naught in Troy Town, and afield
Just fodder to appease the fury of Death,
Who ravens by Scamander.

So we meet
In the deep dawn; and furbish up our arms;
And call one to another, in the dusk,

With hearthside sayings and century-old jests,
Until Æneas and Antenor come,
Our leaders, and with sharp words marshalling us,
Bid sound the trumpet, and the Tymbrian gate
Vomits us **for**th upon the barren plains.

IV

EASTER EVE

" Ses meurtriers donc ses rencontraient de bon cœur "
—ALPHONSE MOREAU.

His murderers met. Their consciences were free:
The sun's eclipse was past, the tumult stilled
In Jewry, and their duty well fulfilled.

Quoth Caiaphas :—*It wrung my heart to see*
His mother's grief, God knows! Yet blasphemy
Was proven, the uprising imminent,
And all the church-supporting element
Demanded action, sir, of you and me.

Quoth Pilate :—*When this Nazarene denied*
Even Cæsar's rule, reluctantly I knew
My duty to the state, sir. Still, I tried,
But found no way, to spare him yet stay true
In loyalty. . . . And still, the poor lad cried,
"Forgive them, for they know not what they do!"

30

V

ST. MAGDALENE

"Femme je suis, ridée, povrette et ancienne'
—Théodore Passerat.

Must I abide forever in this place
Of bloodless folk, amid the vain outcries
Of fools that deem me holy, full of grace,
And skillful in foresaying prophecies?
Thou wouldst not know me in this wrinkled guise—
How couldst thou, O belovèd? I am she
Thou knewest those mad years in Galilee
When we were young. And now thy tale is told,
And I await death, shivering wretchedly,
A pitiful poor woman, shrunk and old.

They call thee god. Paul, when his choleric face
Enkindles from his ever-blazing eyes,
Swears thou art god, and blusters of a place—
A city that the man calls Paradise,—
Wherein thou reignest. Dear, am I not wise
That deem thee worthy of idolatry,
Yet man,—man whom I loved, and verily
Man whom I love, for all that I behold
Thy face no more, belovèd, and I be
A pitiful poor woman, shrunk and old.

31

Yet westerly, where golden clouds enlace
Earth's rim with heaven's, kindlier kingdoms rise;
For there the fortunate Far Islands face
The ends of Ocean, and the sacrifice
Burns ever to Dis' Queen, and no man sighs
In vain for quietude,—where even we
May win such grace of grave Persephonê
As to obliterate woes manifold
In dragging days that fretted sordidly
A pitiful poor woman, shrunk and old.

Man whom I loved, my heart cries out to thee,
All that thou wert I loved!—and so, let be
To dream of maids immortal arms enfold,
Nor rank with Dryopê or Danaë
A pitiful poor woman, shrunk and old.

VI

MARCUS AURELIUS: A SUPPRESSED "MEDITATION"

" L'impératrice a les beaux yeux"
—ANTOINE RICZI.

BRIGHT eyes in truth Faustina hath:
They are colored like that restive path
Which sunset cleaves across the sea;
They are as chill; it well may be
Their splendors, also, do but screen
Waste wreckage and coiled, slow, obscene,
Vague ravenous things. It is of this
I think whenever her lips kiss.

She is brightly colored and soft and frail;
Her beauty like a tinctured veil
Hides and divides her heart from me.

Nor would I vex your secrecy,
Grave eyes, that screen her unguessed heart,
Wherein I ask not any part;
It is enough that ye are bright.

I praise you; and am expedite
Once more to touch Faustina's hair
Caressingly, and note how fair

33

Her body is, which Parcæ planned,
And fashioned fitly, to command
Such love as all men understand.

Grant her unfaithful, and wherein
Am I less favored by Faustine
Than were her heart all faithfulness?

Fools in their folly face distress;
But wisdom muffles wisdom's sight
And looks for naught more recondite
In any woman's grace than this—
Fair flesh, bright hair, and lips that kiss
So winsomely that thereupon
Man's wisdom wins oblivion,
And right and reason, swooning, seem
Faint figments of a fool's fond dream.

VII

AMAIMON VISITS THE THEBAID

"Quam luna adest video nocte illusiones dæmonum"
—ALESSANDRO DE MEDICI.

EACH night at moonrise is let forth from hell
In a fair woman's shape—yea, I know well
How fair it is!—Amaimon; and thus stands
A darkling shade against stilled seas of sands
Made wonderful with moonlight; and speaks not.
    What need?—Amaimon knows I have forgot
No one of those soft curves Amaimon wears.

    So have I need of penance and long prayers:
Because since ever time began to be,
No woman, living, was lovelier than she,
Nor statelier,—yea, buoyant with that power
Her beauty loaned, she moved as moves a flower,
Mire-rooted, nodding by a pool wherein
Its double drowns, and dancing when its twin
Struggles in wind-stirred waters.

                              Nay, most sweet
Of women, I serve that Man whose tortured feet
Spurned Zeus from heaven, and for human sake
Trod evil down, even as folk tread a snake

35

And end all, once for all; by night and day
My prayers assail the ears of God, nor stay
For any bodily weakness till I gain
Surety of pardon through my body's pain.

    Hath God not pardoned me? Men tell of them
That bent with sickness touched my cassock's hem
And straight were hale. They tell how these poor hands
Raised dead folk even. Throughout distant lands
My fame is spread, where emperors quake to tell
Their harlots of some recent miracle
Which I—nay, which High God performed through me
That God's sole glory be proclaimed, and be
A scourge to scoffers.

               So, being fain to die,
I bide that day when High God lifts on high
My soul, and sets me with His cherubim,
Remembering how I have striven for Him
And smitten heresy—yea, with sword and flame
Laid waste how many homes!—in His dear name,
Whose wrath is quenchless.

              It is well with me:
O woman the fiend mimics, how is it with thee?

—With thee, enswirled in some unending sweep
Of ageless flame, whose fires forever leap
Like adders round the damned their coils consume
Not ever, nor relinquish! These illume

Bright tender bodies, such as Cæsar kissed
But yesterday, and now long torment twist. . . .
Ey, what a host of women howl in hell
Who were when they wore flesh so lovable,
And whom men loved as I—

                        But thou art dead,
Rotted, and damned, long since.

                        When I am sped
To Heaven's loftiest courts, and thereamong
Made free of Heaven, how shall I force my tongue
To honor Him that damned thee? and how be
Content with Heaven?   What, through eternity
Hear thy voice—thine, my lost love, loved in vain,
And lost, lost, lost, with only Heaven to gain!—
Hear thy voice call in agony to God,
Who likewise hears—and heeds not!

                        Ey, once shod
With gold and clad in fair white linen cloth,
Shall I then be quite changed? and not be wroth
With God? but be as God is? and never know
Regret for thee, nor pity for the woe
Of shrieking fire-wrapped folk swept to and fro
Where Satan gibes at them and the worm stings?

   Lust, who is overlord of living things;
Lust, by the heavings of whose leathery wings
The flames of hell are fanned to signal-fires
That mark each haven each human heart desires;

Lust, who with ceaseless and illusive snares
Derides our dreams and prompts us in our prayers;
Lust, who is strong and patient and cautelous,
And whom fiends name Amaimon in Satan's house:
Plays thus at dice, our stake being my soul's bliss.

Nay, God is love (Amaimon whispers this),
Nor pedant-like peers from far heaven's vault
To estimate His children's least light fault
As folk weigh gold, to the last hair-breadth's worth.
Grant that this woman, living upon earth,
A little leaned to Marcion's mad creed,
That High God grieves when unbelievers bleed
And Holy Church's servants, or with rod
Or rack or rope, attest the might of God:—
"Because a father's love, pre-eminent
In Him, contrives no curious punishment,
But, even as earthly fathers check a child,
Reproves, and for love's sake is reconciled":—
Thus runneth Marcion's foul heresy.
This woman, then, must burn. It yet may be
All need not burn for all eternity;
And God at last may pardon Donatists,
And Athanasians, and Tritheists—
Ho, even Marcionites,—as lacking wit
Always to read aright God's holy writ,
And, therefore, worthier of pity than hate.
For God is love; and love or soon or late
Forgives,—yea, even pardons thy dread to see
In God some burlier counterpart of thee.

Such blasphemies Amaimon whispers me
Nightly at moonrise: and I answer not.
   What need?— Amaimon knows I have forgot
No one of those soft curves Amaimon wears.

So have I need of penance and long prayers.

VIII

DAME VENUS IN THURINGIA

"Icy je regne, et je m'assemble tous les hommes"
—Théodore Passerat.

Even to the Hörselberg they follow me,
These men Thou couldst not save: the hollow hill
Is thronged with them that have abandoned Thee
To follow her that yet endures, and will
Outlive all tenets. Canst Thou ever still
Our revelry, O Christ? or canst Thou stay
These lips that on my lover's lips I lay,
Deriding Thee unpunished? Nay, God wot,
Here rest no pilgrims on Thy bloodless way,
Where in the Hörselberg we know Thee not!

We have no ending to our revelry;
Of lust and drunkenness we have our fill:
Thou hast the uplands, and the sun-bathed sea—
My mother sea!—is subject to Thy will,
Poor foolish Christ, that hadst not wit to kill
Her whom Thou hadst discrowned. I may not stray
Amid the fields of Paphos, and men pray
No more to me in Eryx; yet no jot
Of lust's old worship dwindles, even to-day,
Where in the Hörselberg we know Thee not.

40

Wilt Thou not slay me for much blasphemy?
Strike and have done! Whom kindlier shouldst Thou kill
Than one begotten of the restive sea,
Thus penned, and turned a potent poison till
Man's folly fail him?—I with futile skill
Snare ceaselessly; and never see the day
Smite huddling golden waves; nor feel the spray
Make glad my lips. My godhood is forgot.
I tread a hill more drear than Golgotha,
Where in the Hörselberg we know Thee not.

Christ, curse me not with immortality!
I once was Aphroditê; must I be
A thing unclean, and unto fools allot
All fools may crave, even for eternity,
Where in the Hörselberg we know Thee not?

IX

ONE END OF LOVE

" Yolande dit, en soupirant"
—ALPHONSE MOREAU.

It is long since we met,—she said.
I answered,—*Yes.*

　　　　　　She is not fair,
But very old now, and no gold
Gleams in that scant gray withered hair
Where once much gold was: and, I think,
Not easily might one bring tears
Into her eyes, which have become
Like dusty glass.

　　　　　'Tis thirty years,
I said.—*And then the war came on
Apace, and our young King had need
Of men to serve him oversea
Against the heathen. For their greed,
Puffed up at Tunis, troubles him—*

　　She said:—*This week my son is gone
To him at Paris with his men.*
And then:—*You never married, John?*

I answered,—*No.* And so we sate
Musing a while.

        Then with his guests
Came Robert; and his thin voice broke
Upon my dream, with the old jests,
No food for laughter now; and swore
We must be friends now that our feud
Was overpast.

        We are grown old,—
Eh, John?—he said. *And, by the Rood!*
'Tis time we were at peace with God
Who are not long for this world.

        —Yea,
I answered;—*we are old.* And then,
Remembering that April day
At Calais, and that hawthorn field
Wherein we fought long since, I said:—
We are friends now.

        And she sate by,
Scarce heeding. Thus the evening sped.

And we ride homeward now, and I
Ride moodily: my palfrey jogs
Along a rock-strewn way the moon
Lights up for us; yonder the bogs

Are curdled with thin ice; the trees
Are naked; from the barren wold
The wind comes like a blade aslant
Across a world grown very old.

X

VILLON QUITS FRANCE

" Demain tous nous mourrons; c'est juste notre affaire"
—THÉODORE PASSERAT.

WE hang to-morrow, then? That doom is fit
For most of us, I think. Yet, harkee, friend,
I have a ballad here which I have writ
Of us and our high ending. Pray you, send
The scrawl to Cayeux, bidding him commend
François to grace. Old Colin loves me well,
For no good reason, save it so befell
We two were young together. . . . When I am hung,
Colin will weep—and then will laugh, and tell
How many pranks we played when we were young.

Dear lads of yesterday! . . . We had not wit
To live always so we might not offend,
Yet—how we laughed! I marvel now at it,
Because that merry company will spend
No more mad nights together. Some are penned
In abbeys, some in dungeons, others fell
In battle. . . . Time assesses death's *gabelle,*—
Salt must be taxed, eh?—well, we ranked among
The salt of earth, once, who are old and tell
How many pranks we played when we were young.

45

Afraid to die, you ask?—Why, not a whit.
Ah, no! whole-heartedly I mean to wend
Out of a world I have found exquisite
By every testing. For I apprehend
Life was not made all lovely to the end
That life ensnare us, nor the miracle
Of youth devised but as a trap to swell
Old Legion's legions; and must give full tongue
To praise no less than prayer, when bidden tell
How many pranks we played when we were young.

Nay, cheerily we of the Cockle-shell,
And all whose youth was nor to stay nor quell,
Will dare foregather when earth's knell is rung,
And Calvary's young conqueror bids us tell
How many pranks we played when we were young.

XI

INVOCATION: TO THE DARK VENUS

"Audite litaniam, quam dulce in noctibus quondam"
—ALESSANDRO DE MEDICI.

HEARKEN and heed, Melænis!
For all that the litany ceased
When Time had pilfered the victim,
And flouted thy pale-lipped priest,
And set astir in the temple
Where burned the fires of thy shrine
The owls and wolves of the desert—
Yet hearken, (*the issue is thine!*)
And let the heart of Atys,
At last, at last, be mine!

For I have followed, nor faltered—
Adrift in a land of dreams
Where laughter and pity and terror
Commingle as confluent streams,
I have seen and adored the Sidonian,
Implacable, fair and divine,—
And bending low, have implored thee
To hearken, (*the issue is thine!*)
And let the heart of Atys,
At last, at last, be mine!

47

There are taller lads than Atys,
And many are wiser than he,—
How should I heed them?—whose fate is
Ever to serve and to be
Ever the lover of Atys,
And die that Atys may dine,
Live if he need me—Then heed me,
And speed me, (*the moment is thine!*)
And let the heart of Atys,
At last, at last, be mine!

HIC TONAT: DEA ADEST

Fair is the form unbeholden,
And golden the glory of thee
Whose voice is the voice of a vision,
Whose face is the foam of the sea,
And the fall of whose feet is the flutter
Of breezes in birches and pine,
When thou drawest near me, to hear me,
And cheer me, (*the moment is thine!*)
And let the heart of Atys,
At last, at last, be mine!

*   *   *   *   *

Long I besought thee, nor vainly,
Daughter of Water and Air,—
Charis! Idalia! Hortensis!
Hast thou not heard the prayer,

When the blood stood still with loving,
And the blood in me leapt like wine,
And I cried on thy name, Melænis?—
That heard me, (*the glory is thine!*)
And let the heart of Atys,
At last, at last, be mine!

Falsely they tell of thy dying,
Thou that art older than Death;
And never the Hörselberg hid thee,
Whatever the slanderer saith;
For the stars are as heralds forerunning,
When laughter and love combine
At twilight, in thy light, Melænis—
That heard me, (*the glory is thine!*)
And let the heart of Atys,
At last, at last, be mine!

XII

RONSARD RE-VOICES A TRUISM

"Quand vous serez bien vieille, et quand je serais mort"
—Théodore Passerat.

When you are very old, and I am gone,
Not to return, it may be you will say—
Hearing my name and holding me as one
Long dead to you,—in some half-jesting way
Of speech, sweet as vague heraldings of May
Rumored in woods when first the throstles sing:—
He loved me once. And straightway murmuring
My half-forgotten rhymes, you will regret
Evanished times when I was wont to sing
So very lightly, *Love runs into debt.*

I shall not heed you then. My course being run
For good or ill, I shall have gone my way,
And know you, love, no longer,—nor the sun,
Perchance, nor any light of earthly day,
Nor any joy nor sorrow,—while at play
The world speeds merrily, nor reckoning
Our coming or our going. Lips will cling,
Forswear, and be forsaken, and men forget
Where once our tombs were, and our children sing—
So very lightly!—*Love runs into debt.*

50

If in the grave love have dominion
Will that wild cry not quicken the wise clay,
And taunt with memories of fond deeds undone—
Some joy untasted, some lost holiday,—
All death's large wisdom? Will that wisdom lay
The ghost of any sweet familiar thing
Come haggard from the Past, or ever bring
Forgetfulness of those two lovers met
When all was April?—nor too wise to sing
So very lightly, *Love runs into debt.*

Yea, though the years of vain remembering
Draw nigh, and age be drear, yet in the spring
We meet and kiss, whatever hour be set
Wherein all hours attain to harvesting,—
So very lightly Love runs into debt.

XIII

JAUNTS FROM STRATFORD

—"Loin de Stratford": Paul Verville.

III—IN VERONA
"Il m'étonne de voir que le vieux Capulet"

I HAD not thought the house of Capulet
Might boast a daughter of such colorful grace
As this whole-hearted girl, with flower-soft face
Round which the glory of her hair is set
Like some great golden halo;—and, as yet,
Love is to her a word that, spoken, spurs
Wonder alone, since love administers
In nothing to the mirth of Juliet.

What if some day I woke this heart unharried
As yet by love, and won these lips more red
Than rain-tossed cherries?—*Look, the dancers go.
What's he that would not dance? If he be married
My grave is like to be my wedding-bed.*
—God rest you, sweet! the knave is Romeo.

XII—IN TROY
"Le Scamandre engourdi, qui la lune illumine"

STAGNANT Scamander, which the moon—a slight
Frail-seeming crescent toiling through gaunt trees

Mid stars that follow her like golden bees,—
Makes glittering; beyond its marge a white
Glitter of tossed bleached bones where camp-dogs fight
For offal, and a glitter of panoplies
Where sentinels prowl; and partly shrouding these,
Thin fever-breeding mists and dubious night.

And one clear song—fond, as all love-songs be—
From Troilus' fevered lips that give fond vent
To love and wonder and idolatry,
Snapped short; and mutterings of thunder, blent
With cries of mourners, and the garrulous glee
Of Cressida in Diomedes' tent.

XIV

INVITATION TO THE VOYAGE

"Quand le poëte d'Angleterre disait que ce monde"
—Paul Verville.

The world's a stage?—Well, faith! it may have
   seemed so
In days less bleak when Arden's brakes were green,
And Rosalind's low insolent fond laughter
Woke mirth to charm that planet, which to-day
Seems all one vast decorous hospital,—
Germless, immaculate, well-ventilated,
Whitewashed, and odorful with antiseptics.
   And we that toss upon the softest beds,
While yet our fever lasts, are impotent
Beneath this dreary burden of right angles
And blank white walls. And so, we twist, and murmur,
And groan, and twitch the coverlets awry,
Which Mrs. Grundy, head-nurse of our ward,
Pats straight again, in courtesying to the doctor.
   Lean Dr. Death, who never lost a case,
Comes thus; and daily pauses by one's bed;
Fingers the pulse; declares the fever abating;
Writes a prescription for the apothecary,
Old Time; then cuts a jest or so,—departing
With dubious promises of one's discharge
Next year, next month, next week, may be.

54

                                        Ha, neighbor,
Slim pale-haired woman with opal-colored eyes,
Why bide his pleasure? Nay, let us steal out
Together, and—blithe mariners faring forth
On chartless seas,—seek out a vessel bound
For some politer port, made point-device
By Fragonard, Watteau, or whom you will
So the contriver of this hospital
Be not the architect.

                              Oh, dimly gleams
Our haven; for its ways are vaporous
With smouldering incense, mid whose loitering spirals
Frail cupids weave, eternally, long garlands
Of ribbons and pale roses,—weave unvexed
By any garish sunlight, since one star
Alone peeps out of heaven. See, the moon
Shows like a silver sickle in the east,
But casts no shadows yet; and twilight dims
All glow of color where resistless gallants,
Sleek abbés, and false subtle lovely women
Pass to the sound of tinkling mandolines
And hushed contralto laughter.

                                 We will make
Rondeaux of life and triolets of death;
And be at peace; and never laugh aloud;
And grieve not though he mar those stately hedges
Wherethrough he leers—gaunt sensual Pierrot!—
To note the ankles of young Columbine.

Yes, we will smile to see her pirouette
With Harlequin in shadowed avenues,—
Yew-shadowed statue-haunted avenues,
Where pensive gods yet dream of Jeanne Vaubernier,—
While tricked Pierrot sings at her father's window;—
Smile it may be, but never laugh aloud. . . .
And in the autumn Columbine will die,
And Harlequin be sad a whole half-hour.
But Pierrot's heart will break; and he will grieve
That so much earth lies heavily on her
Who trod the earth so lightly!—and will weep
Big facile tears, and babble to the moon.

Will you not go?—Then come. Give me your hand,—
That firm small slender hand. Tread quietly,
For Mrs. Grundy nods now, who will wake
Full-cry when all our fellow-patients chatter
And drone and bustle like fat surfeited flies
Round our dead reputations.

Let us go.

XV

THE HOIDENS

"Au point du premier jour, dans l'enfance du tout"
—Antoine Riczi.

WHEN the Morning broke before us
Came the wayward Three astraying,
Chattering in babbling chorus,
(Obloquies of Æther saying),—
Hoidens that, at pegtop playing,
Flung their Top where yet it whirls
Through the coil of clouds unstaying;
For the Fates are captious girls.

CLOTHO

Why, upon that Toy before us
Insects cluster! Hear them saying,
In the quaintest shrillest chorus:—
'Life affords no time for playing!
And for each that goes astraying,
Featly as a planet whirls
Drops the stroke of doom unstaying,
For the Fates are captious girls.'

LACHESIS

La, I thought it reeled before us
Tumbling, lurching, stumbling, straying,

57

In some sort of mumbling chorus!
Now I see them at their playing—
I too see,—and hear them saying:—
'Note with what fixed aim life whirls
Onward to set goals unstaying,
For the Fates are captious girls.'

ATROPOS

Sisters, I am tired of straying.
Catch the Toy while yet it whirls!
Cleanse the Toy, and end our playing!

—For the Fates are captious girls.

HORTENSIS

" Mort, j'appelle de ta rigueur "

I

ACCORDING TO THEIR FOLLY

"Ce que vous faites-là n'importe pas"
—Charles Garnier.

Ye that made merry through mirthless ages,
And jeered in the thick of the knights' mêlée,
And derided all wrangles of sophists and sages,
And toasted your toes round an auto-da-fé,—
Do ye grieve, in your coffins, now worms assay
That motley logic of quip and pun
And elvish laughter?—or still do ye say,
Whatever ye do there matters to none?

Chuckling and shrugging, ye clutched such wages
As life allotted; then went your way
Into the dark, where no conflict rages,
No wrangles follow, no cruelties stray.
—Le Glorieux, Armstrong, Patch, Brusquet,
And Sommers! rest ye, for jesting is done,
And ye need not joke now as yesterday,
For whatever ye do there matters to none.

And a dream that he found in his tomb assuages
The brutish sorrows of Triboulet;
And Dagonet sleeps, and no more engages

To follow his master in any fray;
And CHICOT, too, makes his bed of clay—
Whither wins never the Gascon sun,—
Where baubles and sceptres alike decay,
And whatever ye do there matters to none.

   My prince! it is better to quote than obey
The precepts of Solon and Solomon;
Yet the world they admonished is larger than they,
And whatever ye do there matters to none.

II

FOOT-NOTE FOR IDYLS

"Le Sicilien chantait—mais c'est, ma foy, bien drôle"
—Théodore Passerat.

'Mongst all immortals tardiest is their tread!
Dear and desired, they tread with dainty feet,
By whose dear advent all are comforted
'Mongst mortal men! Thus, thus, thy verses greet
The Coming Hours—those Hours that from the heat
And mirth and friendly girls of Sicily,
Unheeding, haled thee to hell's minstrels'-seat,
To edify austere Persephonê.

The living may forget; only the dead
Are hopeless! sang blithe Corydon, where beat
Bright waves upon bright sands, and overhead
Pines murmured benisons. Now is it sweet
To rhyme of this in thy less glad retreat,
Theocritus, who badest that song be
Immortal? and dost thou find that song meet
To edify austere Persephonê?

Now all old hours and all old years are sped
What profits it with thee if men repeat

Or all or anything thy live lips said?
Thou hast forgot Bombyca's *ivory feet,*
The shrill cicalæ's chirp, the lambkins' bleat,
And Lacon's *honied song on Helykê.*
What profits thee the honied sound of it
To edify austere Persephonê?

Lord of glad songs, for us the winding-sheet,
For thee the funeral pyre—*built near the sea,*—
Bids singing cease, and songless lips compete
To edify austere Persephonê.

❧

III

THE GOD-FATHER

"Primus in orbe deos fecit timor; ardua cœlo"
—Caius Petronius Arbiter.

Always was fear the god's ambassador,
Since first in traverse of high-tumbling seas
Man quailed and out of thunderings made Thor;
Or mid the desert's dumb infinities
He shuddered, dreaming of Tanith and the Sphinx;
Or noting life's large cruelty, surmised
Plethoric Zeus, with twinkling eyes that roam
Alcmena-ward.—Still as man fears, man thinks;
And presently each dread is canonized,
And duly terror is wheedled and exorcised,
And given his priest, and shrine, and hecatomb.

Fearing, we loathe, and to the thing abhorred
Bow down; and terror and fancy beget a god
A while evaded, and a while adored,
And afterward bemocked. As with a rod
Time smote the lords of Nineveh and Khem,
And raised the dreams which Hellas deemed divine;
As presently the grosser gods of Rome
Turned ghost, and Saturn's pilfered diadem

65

Rolled at Christ's bleeding feet.—What praise was thine
That art most feared of all? what gilded shrine,
Cajoling priest, and steaming hecatomb?

  Scant need to wheedle Death! men said. Our life,
With all the pain and passion of the whole,
With all the toil, the sorrow and the strife,
Is but a passing onward to the goal
Where Death awaits us. Mid his votaries
Our birth-cry ranked us; nor may any art
Avail to save us, while the years consume
As ashes smoulder when their fervor dies
Insensibly; and he that lies apart
In darkness hears the pulsing of Death's heart,
And knows that Death waits near him in the gloom.

  Yea, of all gods thou only lovest not gifts!
Others we placate; or in smiting we
Evade them. When thou smitest with what shifts
May we evade thee? or how placate thee?—
Thou wilt not hearken to any prayer of ours;
Thou biddest emperors and popes as well
As witless clowns, *Be still and bide thy fate!*—
Whose altar we have wreathed with fitting flowers—
With purple lupine, crumpled poppy-bell,
Ambiguous mandrake, and pale asphodel—
Since praise thee or blame thee, thou art obdurate.

  And nor to wheedle thee, nor to demand
Favor of thee or any pity of thee,

We come. Beneath a lifted sword we stand
And praise thee, knowing whatever gods may be
Thy altar is not shaken: though the creeds
And outworn faiths of dreaming seer and priest
Endure as sinister shadows, or endure
As marsh fires glittering round a path that leads
Nowhither; and the night be, and the east
Sleep, and the sun not waken;—yet at least,
Though all things else be doubtful, death is sure.

We praise thee, knowing how vainly fancy spans
With timorous dreams the grave's unplumbed abyss.
Vainly we famed the calm Olympians,
And vainly Ammon-Ra, and Artemis,
And Neith, and Krishna. Comfort we have had
Of kindlier lords whose fabled potency
With shadows decked the darkness lest the dread
Of darkness absolute should drive us mad,—
But Time discrowns them. Time endures. But he
Discrowns thee never, and endures by thee
Endured, against that time when Time be dead.

IV

BALLAD OF THE DESTROYER

"Ainsi nous applaudons la mort, la mort qui vient"
—Nicolas de Caen.

WE laud him thus, that comes unto the king,
And lightly plucks him from the cushioned throne;
And drowns his glory and his warfaring
In unrecorded dim oblivion;
And girds another with the sword thereof;
And sets another in his stead to reign;
And ousts the remnant, nakedly to gain
Styx' formless shore and nakedly complain
Midst twittering ghosts lamenting life and love.

For Death is merciless: a crack-brained king
He raises in the place of Prester John,
Smites Priam, and mid-course in conquering
Bids Cæsar pause; the wit of Solomon,
The wealth of Nero and the pride thereof,
And battle-prowess—or of Tamburlaine,
Darius, Jeshua, or Charlemaigne,—
Wheedle and bribe and surfeit Death in vain,
And get no grace of him nor any love.

Incuriously he smites the armored king
And tricks his counsellors ;—as, later on,
Death will, half-idly, still our pleasuring,
And change for fevered laughter in the sun
Sleep such as Merlin's,—and excess thereof,—
Whence we, divorceless Death our Viviaine
Implacable, may never more regain
The unforgotten rapture, and the pain
And grief and ecstasy of life and love.

For, presently, as quiet as the king
Sleeps now that planned the keeps of Ilion,
We, too, will sleep, whilst overhead the spring
Rules, and young lovers laugh—as we have done,—
And kiss—as we, that take no heed thereof,
But slumber very soundly, and disdain
The world-wide heralding of winter's wane
And swift sweet ripple of the April rain
Running about the world to waken love.

We shall have done with love, and Death be king
And turn our nimble bodies carrion,
Our red lips dusty ;—yet our live lips cling
Despite that age-long severance, and are one
Despite the grave and the vain grief thereof,—
Which we will baffle, if in Death's domain
Fond memories may enter, and we twain
May dream a little, and rehearse again
In that unending sleep our present love.

Speed forth to her in halting unison,
My rhymes; and say no hindrance may restrain
Love from his aim when Love is bent thereon;
And that were love at my disposal lain—
All mine to take!—and Death had said, *Refrain,*
Lest I, even I, exact the cost thereof,
I know that even as the weather-vane
Follows the wind so would I follow Love.

V

EXHORTATION TOWARD ALMSGIVING

"Faulse beaulté, qui tant me couste cher"
—François Villon.

O BEAUTY of her, whereby I am undone!
O Grace of her, that hath no grace for me!
O Love of her, the bit that guides me on
To sorrow and to grievous misery!
O felon Charms, my poor heart's enemy!
O furtive murderous Pride! O pitiless, great,
Cold Eyes of her! have done with cruelty!
Have pity upon me ere it be too late!

Happier for me if elsewhere I had gone
For pity,—ah, far happier for me,
Since never of her may any grace be won,
And lest dishonor slay me, I must flee.
Haro! I cry, (and cry how uselessly!)
Haro! I cry to folk of all estate,
For I must die unless it chance that she
Have pity upon me ere it be too late.

M'ayme, that day in whose disastrous sun
Your beauty's flower must fade and wane and be
No longer beautiful, draws near,—whereon

71

I will nor plead nor mock;—not I, for we
Shall both be old and vigorless! M'ayme,
Drink deep of love, drink deep, nor hesitate
Until the spring run dry, but speedily
Have pity upon me—ere it be too late!

Lord Love, that all love's lordship hast in fee,
Lighten, ah, lighten thy displeasure's weight,
For all true hearts should, of Christ's charity,
Have pity upon me ere it be too late.

VI

COMFORT FOR CENTENARIANS

—After Nicolas de Caen.

Marvel not if my words are bold;
Though the sound be rude, yet the sense is true:
Too long you have flouted a tale oft-told
By the stammering tongues of men that woo,
And woo you vainly. Your brain is askew
For pride in your body's magnificence,
And its color and curving so fair to view;—
And what will it matter a hundred years hence?

My burden, I grant you, is blunt and old:
Yet time will sharpen its sting when you—
Even you yourself!—and the things you hold
At so dear a price are a bone or two;
And those wonderful eyes, whose heaven-like blue
Is the crown of your beauty's excellence,
Are unsavory holes that a worm crawls through;—
And what will it matter a hundred years hence?

Encrusted and tainted with churchyard mould,
Your dear perfections must lie perdue;
Take on such favor as few behold

73

With liking, and certainly none pursue;
And your beauty be reft of all revenue,
And suffer the blind worm's insolence,
Who recks not at all of height, hair and hue,—
And what will it matter a hundred years hence?

ETTARRE, I proffer my love anew,
And life with a jest at the world's expense;
And if for your favor I vainly sue—
Why, what will it matter a hundred years hence?

VII

THE CONQUEROR PASSES

" Non dormatz plus! les messatges de douz pascor "
—RAIMBAUT DE VAQUEIRAS.

AWAKEN! for the servitors of Spring
Proclaim his triumph! ah, make haste to see
With what tempestuous pageantry they bring
The victor homeward! haste, for this is he
That cast out Winter, and all woes that cling
To Winter's garments, and bade April be!

And now that Spring is master, let us be
Content, and laugh as anciently in spring
The battle-wearied Tristran laughed, when he
Was come again Tintagel-ward, to bring
Glad news of Arthur's victory—and see
Ysoude, with parted lips, that waver and cling.

Not yet in Brittany must Tristran cling
To this or that sad memory, and be
Alone, as she in Cornwall; for in spring
Love sows against far harvestings,—and he
Is blind, and scatters baleful seed that bring
Such fruitage as blind Love lacks eyes to see.

Love sows, but lovers reap: and ye will see
The loved eyes lighten, feel the loved lips cling,
Never again when in the grave ye be
Incurious of your happiness in spring,
And get no grace of Love there, whither he
That bartered life for love no love may bring.

No braggart Heracles avails to bring
Alcestis hence; nor here may Roland see
The eyes of Aude; nor here the wakening spring
Vex any man with memories: for there be
No memories that cling as cerements cling,
No force that baffles Death, more strong than he.

Us hath he noted, and for us hath he
An hour appointed; and that hour will bring
Oblivion.—Then laugh! Laugh, dear, and see
The tyrant mocked, while yet our bosoms cling,
While yet our lips obey us, and we be
Untrammeled in our little hour of spring!

Thus in the spring we jeer at Death, though he
Will see our children perish, and will bring
Asunder all that cling while love may be.

VIII

THE MENDICANTS

"Domna, de totz bos aips complida"
—RAIMBAUT DE VAQUEIRAS.

O MADAM Destiny, omnipotent,
Be not too obdurate to us who pray
That this thy transient grant of youth be spent
In laughter as befits a holiday,—
From which the evening summons us away,
From which to-morrow wakens us to strife
And toil and grief and wisdom,—and to-day
Grudge us not life!

O Madam Destiny, omnipotent,
Why need our elders trouble us at play?
We know that very soon we shall repent
The idle follies of our holiday,
And being old, shall be as wise as they:
But now we are not wise, and lute and fife
Plead sweetlier than axioms,—so to-day
Grudge us not life!

O Madam Destiny, omnipotent,
You have given us youth—and must we cast away
The cup undrained and our one coin unspent

Because our elders' beards and hearts are gray?
They have forgotten that if we delay
Death claps us on the shoulder, and with knife
Or cord or fever, flouts the prayer we pray—
Grudge us not life!

Madam, recall that in the sun we play
But for an hour, then have the worm for wife,
The tomb for habitation,—and to-day
Grudge us not life!

IX

ALONE IN APRIL

" In un boschetto trovai pastorella"
—ALESSANDRO DE MEDICI.

RUSTLING leaves of the willow-tree
Peering downward at you and me,
And no man else in the world to see.

Only the birds, whose dusty coats
Show dark in the green—whose throbbing throats
Turn joy to music and love to notes.

Lean your body against the tree,
Lifting your red lips up to me,
Ettarre, and kiss, with no man to see!

And let us laugh for a little.—Yea,
Let love and laughter herald the day
When laughter and love will be put away.

Then you will remember the willow-tree
And this very hour, and remember me,
Ettarre,—whose face you will no more see!

79

So swift, so swift the glad time goes,
And Eld and Death with their countless woes
Draw near, and the end thereof no man knows.

Lean your body against the tree,
Lifting your red lips up to me,
Ettarre, and kiss, with no man to see!

X

"—BUT WISDOM IS JUSTIFIED OF HER CHILDREN"

"Oramai quando flore"
—ALESSANDRO DE MEDICI.

PHYLLIDA, spring wakes about us—
Wakes to mock at us and flout us
That so coldly do delay:
When the very birds are mating,
Pray you, why should we be waiting—
We that might be wed to-day?

Life is brief, the wise men tell us;—
Even those dusty, musty fellows
That have done with life,—and pass
Where the wraith of Aristotle
Hankers, vainly, for a bottle,
Youth and some frank Grecian lass.

Ah, I warrant you;—and Zeno
Would not reason, now, could he know
One more chance to live and love:
For, at best, the merry Maytime
Is a very fleeting playtime;—
Why, then, waste an hour thereof?

Plato, Solon, Periander,
Seneca, Anaximander,
Pyrrho, and Parmenides!
Were one hour alone remaining
Would ye spend it in attaining
Learning, or to lips like these?

Thus, I demonstrate by reason
Now is our predestined season
For the garnering of all bliss;
Prudence is but long-faced folly;
Cry a fig for melancholy!
Seal the bargain with a kiss.

XI

THE LOVERS' DOXOLOGY

"O voi che per la via d'amor passate"
—ALESSANDRO DE MEDICI.

LISTEN, all lovers! the spring is here,
And the world is not amiss;
As long as laughter is good to hear,
And lips are good to kiss,—
As long as Youth and Spring endure,—
There is never an evil past a cure,
And the world is never amiss.

O lovers all, I bid ye declare
The world is a pleasant place;—
Give thanks to God for the gift so fair,
Give thanks for His singular grace!
Give thanks for Youth and Love and Spring!
Give thanks, as gentlefolk should, and sing,
The world is a pleasant place!

XII

OF ANNUAL MAGIC: AT TWENTY

"Be m play lo dous temp de pascor"
—Raimbaut de Vaqueiras.

Now I loiter, and dream to the branches' swaying
In furtive conference,—high overhead,—
Atingle with rumors that Winter is spéd
And over his ruins a world goes maying.

Somewhere—impressively,—people are saying
Intelligent things (which their grandmothers said),
While I loiter, and dream to the branches' swaying
In furtive conference, high overhead.

Here the hand of April, unwashed from slaying
Earth's fallen tyrant—for Winter is dead,—
Uncloses anemones, staining them red;
And her daffodils guard me, in squads,—displaying
Intrepid lances lest wisdom tread
Where I loiter and dream to the branches' swaying.

XIII

OF ANNUAL MAGIC: AT TWENTY-FIVE

"Quant erba vertz e fuelha par"
—Raimbaut de Vaqueiras.

April wakes, and the gifts are good
Which April grants in this lonely wood,
Mid the wistful sounds of a solitude
Whose immemorial murmuring
Is the voice of Spring
And murmurs the burden of burgeoning.

April wakes, and her heart is high,
For the Bassarids and the Fauns are nigh,
And prosperous leaves lisp busily
Over fluttered brakes, whence the breezes bring
Vext twittering
To swell the burden of burgeoning.

April wakes, and afield, astray,
She calls to whom at the end I say,
Heart o' My Heart, I am thine alway,—
And I follow, follow her carolling,
For I hear her sing
Above the burden of burgeoning.

85

April wakes ;—it were good to live
(*Yet April passes*), though April give
No other gift for our pleasuring
Than the old, old burden of burgeoning.

XIV

OF ANNUAL MAGIC: AT THIRTY

"Ai! chant d'auzel comensa sa sazos"
—RAIMBAUT DE VAQUEIRAS.

Now May awakes, and spring comes back;
Now green fire creeps from tree to tree,
And he that travels need not lack
The sight of an anemone
'Twixt one sea and another sea;
Now blithe birds build, and wan hearts quicken,
Oblivious of dreams that sicken
Drear ice-engirdled reverie.

Now I in part forget . . . . recall
In part . . . . how yonder throstle's call
Inveigles whither mirth is,—
Because so many lips have told
The tale I told once, who am old,
However young the earth is.

XV

THE DOTARD CONJURER

"Le Printemps est devenu comme un sorcier faible"
—Paul Verville.

Spring is become a dotard conjurer,
And his old magic works not any more!
No more avails the whisper of friendly leaves;
And now the forest is undenizened
Of daydreams, which, like elfin outlaws, once
Lay hid in wait for every passer-by
And pilfered all his sorrows; dawn abates
In wonder and tells flatly, *It is day*,
And tells no more than that now; and the night
Brews no more philtres; and the moon forgets
That ancient wizardry which once was hers.

Ah, the old magic works not any more,
Though I have known its potency. Perchance,
Somewhere a great way off, in Avalon,
Atlantis, or the hushed Hesperides,
Hearts lighten with the coming in of spring,
Even as once. Yes, for this thing has been,
And may be yet in far-off Avalon.

88

For it may be in far-off Avalon,
Even as once—was it not yesterday?—
All forests are akin to Brocelaunde,
And fear and beauty keep their heritage
And breathe of something hidden in the woods
Save birds, and trees, and flowers, and ravenous gnats,—
For they are haunted by those messengers
That April sends about our woods no more
On primal errands. But in Avalon,
Fern-carpeted untroubled Avalon,
When April wakes and rises, with wind-blown hair
And steadfast eyes—when at the tip of the world
The sun takes heart a little,—then sturdy April
Exults, and summons tricksy ministers
To color and curve, like skillful artizans,
The first flush of the apple-blossoms, and marshal
The stout spears of the daffodils, and guide
Frail baby clouds about the lonely heavens;
And polish frost-nipped stars; and re-awaken
Warm gracious land-winds where the restive waters
Shout to the glistening sands and hunger all night
With impotent desire of the naked moon.

Yes; this may be, in far-off Avalon.

Here the old magic works not any more:
And Spring, a dotard conjurer, forgets
The runes and sorceries of yesterday,
And may at best evoke but tenuous visions,—
Faint-hearted dreams that people the turbid past

With half-seen faces and derisive laughter;—
And there is nothing hidden in the woods
Save birds, and trees, and flowers, and ravenous gnats,
And, under all, dead and decaying leaves.

Nay, under all, dead and decaying leaves
Enrich that mould which bred them, and whereby
The tree is nourished and new leaves put forth.

SCOTEIA

"De moy, pauvre, je veuil parler"

I

UNCHARTED

" Une royaume nous cherchons "
—Antoine Riczi.

THERE is a land those hereabout
Ignore. . . . Its gates are barred
By Titan twins, named Fear and Doubt.
These mercifully guard
That land we seek—the land so fair!—
And all the fields thereof,
Where daffodils flaunt everywhere
And ouzels chant of love,—
Lest we attain the Middle-Land,
Whence clouded well-springs rise,
And vipers from a slimy strand
Lift glittering cold eyes.

NOW, THE PARABLE ALL MAY UNDERSTAND,
AND SURELY YOU KNOW THE NAME OF THE LAND!
AH, NEVER A GUIDE OR EVER A CHART
MAY SAFELY LEAD YOU ABOUT THIS LAND,—
THE LAND OF THE HUMAN HEART!

II

SCHOOL-SONG

" Je fais attention aux maîtres "
—ALPHONSE MOREAU.

I have to heed my teachers,
And try to trust my school,
And yet no less, through awkwardness,
Infringe on every rule.

Dim laws I may not understand
I strive to keep—and break,
Somehow;—and see forbidden me
Much that I want—and take
Sometimes;—not meaning to do wrong,
Nor, surely, to deny
The weight of rules one ridicules—
Somewhat,—yet lives thereby.

If teachers could but recollect
The lads they used to be,
I think that all could half-recall,
Somewhere, someone like me.
(*The lads they were!* What looking-glass
Shows me a lad to-day?

With nothing learned, much half-discerned,
I toil already gray).

    Yet honor, ruefully, the rule—
All teachers must be sure
That each mistake their pupils make
Was never known before:
And honor, tacitly, the rule—
No pupil ever thrives
Who questions *Why?* of laws whereby
We lead our ordered lives.

    For we must heed our teachers,
And try to trust our school,
Until they teach the reason each
Infringes every rule.

III

"AS IT WAS IN THE BEGINNING"

Man's love hath many prompters,
But a woman's love hath none;
And he may woo a nimble wit
Or hair that shames the sun,
Whilst she must pick of all one man
And ever brood thereon,—
And for no reason,
And not rightly,—

Save that the plan was foreordained
(More old than Chalcedon,
Or any tower of Tarshish
Or of gleaming Babylon),
That she must love unwillingly
And love till life be done,—
He for a season,
And more lightly.

IV

BALLAD OF THE DOUBLE-SOUL

"Les Dieux, qui trop aiment ses facéties cruelles"
—PAUL VERVILLE.

IN the beginning the Gods made man, and fashioned
the sky and the sea,
And the earth's fair face for man's dwelling-place; and
this was the Gods' decree:—

*Lo, We have given to man five wits: he discerneth folly
and sin;*
*He is swift to deride all the world outside, and blind
to the world within:*
*So that man may make sport and amuse Us, in battling
for phrases or pelf,*
*Now that each may know what forebodeth woe to his
neighbor, and not to himself.*

Yet some have the Gods forgotten,—or is it that subtler
mirth
The Gods extort of a certain sort of folk that cumber the
earth?

FOR THIS IS THE SONG OF THE DOUBLE-SOUL, DISTORTEDLY
TWO IN ONE,—
OF THE WEARIED EYES THAT STILL BEHOLD THE FRUIT
ERE THE SEED BE SOWN,
AND DERIVE AFFRIGHT FOR THE NEARING NIGHT FROM THE
LIGHT OF THE NOONTIDE SUN.

For, one that with hope in the morning set forth, and
knew never a fear,
They have linked with another whom omens bother; and
he whispers in one's ear.

And one is fain to be climbing where only angels have
trod,
But is fettered and tied to another's side who fears that
it might look odd.
And one would worship a woman whom all perfections
dower,
But the other smiles at transparent wiles; and he quotes
from Schopenhauer.

Thus two by two we wrangle and blunder about the
earth,
And that body we share we may not spare; but the
Gods have need of mirth.

SO THIS IS THE SONG OF THE DOUBLE-SOUL, DISTORTEDLY
    TWO IN ONE,—
OF THE WEARIED EYES THAT STILL BEHOLD THE FRUIT
    ERE THE SEED BE SOWN,
AND DERIVE AFFRIGHT FOR THE NEARING NIGHT FROM THE
    LIGHT OF THE NOONTIDE SUN.

V

WHEN TRAVELLERS RETURN

—A fancy from ALPHONSE MOREAU.

THERE is more in this room than is corporal,—
Grieved, silent, and striving in nameless ways,
While I read, with my back against the wall,
And nothing happens, and naught betrays
Unseen sad eyes that are weighing me
Somehow.

　　　They trouble me, too, although
By rule and reason this should not be . . . .

But a woman died here, years ago,
Who loved me much :—and what if the dead
Were doomed to this as their punishment—
That with those whom, living, they loved they tread
Forever, and are omniscient ?

VI

ANNALS

I—"Quis Desiderio?"
(May 15th, 1913)

THERE is no room for grief when harvest nears
And, labor done, fit wages are received,—
No room for grief now that she wins full-sheaved
Her harvest, and no need of any tears.
She goes to garner honorable years;
She was a little wearied by long strife,
And still alert, and still in love with life-—
As ever—would ascend to her compeers.

There is no room for grief; as to its nest
A seabird moves on pinions sure and strong,
Her sturdy spirit mounts when sturdiest,
And life ends nobly like a rounded song.
There is no room for grief; she is at rest
To whom rest was a stranger overlong.

II—"Sed Risit Midas"

(1915: Somewhere in the United States)

Let all I touch be gold! King Midas cried
Of old in Phrygia. Jove heard the prayer,
And Midas laughed; for gold gleamed everywhere
His fingers reached; and iron gleamed outside.

Within, no friendly handclasp might abide
That touch which turned all gold, and made his food
Chill metal on his lips; and plenitude
Derided him. So Midas laughed, and died.

To-day who follows Midas?—*Nay, let be
To whisper of lost friends I knew of old
When England gave me life which France made free!
I trade unbiased; and my guns are sold—
Whoever buys—now all need buy of me,
And all I touch or handle turns to gold!*

III—"Aprilis Gesta"

(Easter, 1865—Easter, 1915: Richmond, Virginia)

*A long half-century since when April reigned,
As now, our cause was lost because unjust—
Else wherefore lost?—when level with the dust
Fell citadels our fathers' faith maintained
Till that old April,—hath the fool ordained,
Imprisoned by his bookshelves; and forgets*

Truth is not lightly slain with bayonets,
Or warfare lost whence honor comes unstained.

And April craved her jest ere time began,—
So time anew brings April, to deride
More changeful, strife-drowned Earth, wherein to span
The surge of war's inexorable tide
Attends the wit of a Virginian,
And men acclaim the Christ men crucified.

IV—"Lex Scripta Est"
(February 14th, 1916)

Time rounds a twelvemonth since you died,—most dear
And brave of women!—and he thrives as yet
Whose craven heart found courage to beget
The lie that slew you;—who, with fame made clear
And past his poison, rest till High God hear
Our prayer, and smite with godlike plenitude
This lean gray snake, and spill the venom spewed
In vain to guard his lewd blood-brother's bier.

Not yet—most dear and brave!—may faith foretell
Fate's fixed inevitable hour, nor be
Rewarded by its advent, to compel
This liar's exile from all less vile than he,
And startle in the loneliest nook of hell
Iscariot and Cain with company.

VII

THE PERFECT REASON

"Le Roy Jésus crucifié"
—ANTOINE RICZI.

KING JESUS hung upon the Cross,
And have ye sinned?—quo' He,—
Nay, Dysmas, 'tis no honest loss
When Satan cogs the dice ye toss,
And thou shalt sup with Me,—
Sedebis apud angelos,
Quia amavisti!

At Heaven's Gate was Heaven's Queen,
And have ye sinned?—quo' She,—
And would I hold him worth a bean
That durst not seek, because unclean,
My cleansing charity?—
Speak thou, that wast the Magdalene,
Quia amavisti!

VIII

TWO IN TWILIGHT

"Ave, Maria, que l'amour Divine inspire"
—ANTOINE RICZI.

I—ALBA

Ave, Maria! whom Love did move
To triumph over earthly love.

Mother and Maid, now that wan stars take flight,
And larks with song assail high heaven's height,
Unwillingly we lose the kindly night
That sheltered us when we were fain thereof.

For we are frail, and know not of His aim,
Yet Whosoever made us—were His name
Jove or Jehovah,—should we dare to blame
Our Maker that He made us fit for love?—

Were we not modeled by an Artizan
That to His liking shaped the soul of man,
And fashioned all things after His own plan,
Divulging nothing of the aims thereof?—

105

Is it by His grace we grow adventurous,
And, laughing, say:—*Love proves victorious,—*
Who made love potent? if love hoodwink us
How may we dare reprove Him That made love?

MATER, ORA FILIUM,
UT POST HOC EXILIUM
NOBIS DONET GAUDIUM
BEATORUM OMNIUM!

II—Serena

Ave, Maria! now cry we so
That see night wake and daylight go.

Mother and Maid, in nothing incomplete,
This night that gathers is more light and fleet
Than twilight trod alway with stumbling feet,
Agentes semper uno animo.

Ever we touch the prize we dare not take!
Ever we know that thirst we dare not slake!
Yet ever to a dreamed-of goal we make—
Est tui cœli in palatio!

Long, long the road, and set with many a snare;
And to how small sure knowledge are we heir
That blindly tread, with twilight everywhere!
Volo in toto; sed non valeo!

Long, long the road, and very frail are we,
That may not lightly curb mortality,
Nor lightly tread together steadfastly,
Et parvum carmen unum facio:—

MATER, ORA FILIUM,
UT POST HOC EXILIUM
NOBIS DONET GAUDIUM
BEATORUM OMNIUM!

IX

NOSTALGIA

—After Alphonse Moreau.

Were the All-Mother wise, life (shaped anotherwise)
Would be all high and true;
Could I be otherwise I had been otherwise
Simply because of you. . . .
With whom I have naught to do,
And who are no longer you!

Life with its pay to be bade us essay to be
What we became,—I believe
Were there a way to be what it was play to be
I would not greatly grieve. . . .
Hearts are not worn on the sleeve.
Let us neither laugh nor grieve!

BUT, OH, THE WORLD IS WIDE, DEAR LASS,
THAT I MUST WANDER THROUGH,
AND MANY A WIND AND TIDE, DEAR LASS,
MUST FLOW 'TWIXT ME AND YOU,
ERE LOVE THAT MAY NOT BE DENIED
SHALL BRING ME BACK TO YOU,
—DEAR LASS!
SHALL BRING ME BACK TO YOU.

X

STY-SONG

—After Nicolas de Caen.

As with her dupes dealt Circê,
Life deals with hers, for she
Reshapes them without mercy,
And shapes them swinishly,
To wallow swinishly,
And for eternity;—

Though, harder than the witch was,
Life, changing not the whole,
Transmutes the body, which was
Proud garment of the soul,
And briefly drugs the soul,
Whose ruin is her goal;—

And means by this thereafter
A subtler mirth to get,
And mock with bitterer laughter
Her helpless dupes' regret,
Their swinish dull regret
For what they half forget.

✤

109

XI

THE TOY-MAKER

From the dawn of the day to the dusk he toiled,
Shaping fanciful playthings with tireless hands,—
Useless trumpery toys; and, with vaulting heart,
Gave them unto all peoples—who mocked at him,
Trampled on them, and soiled them, and went their way.

Then he toiled from the morn to the dusk again,
Gave his gimcracks to people who mocked at him,
Trampled on them, deriding, and went their way.

Thus he labors, and loudly they jeer at him;—
That is, when they remember he still exists.

Who, you ask, *is this fellow?*—What matter names?
He is only a scribbler who is content.

XII

THE CASTLE OF CONTENT

—Provençal Burden.

Through the mist of years does it gleam as yet—
That fair and free extent
Of moonlit turret and parapet,
Which castled, once, Content?

> *Ei ho! Ei ho! the Castle of Content,*
> *With drowsy music drowning merriment*
> *Where Dreams and Visions held high carnival,*
> *And frolicking frail Loves made light of all,—*
> *Ei ho! the vanished Castle of Content!*

Such toll we took of his niggling Hours
That the troops of Time were sent
To seize the treasures and fell the towers
Of the Castle of Content.

> *Ei ho! Ei ho! the Castle of Content,*
> *With flaming roof and tumbling battlement*
> *Where Time hath conquered, and the firelight*
>   *streams*
> *Above sore-wounded Loves and dying Dreams,—*
> *Ei ho! the vanished Castle of Content!*

The towers are fallen; no laughter rings
Through the rafters, charred and rent;
The ruin is wrought of all goodly things
In the Castle of Content.

> *Ei ho! Ei ho! the Castle of Content,*
> *Razed in the Land of Youth, where mirth was*
>   *meant!*
> *Nay, all is ashes there; and all in vain*
> *Hand-shadowed eyes turn backward, to regain*
> *Disastrous memories of that dear domain,—*
> *Ei ho! the vanished Castle of Content!*

XIII

THE PARODIST

—After Paul Verville.

I HEAR proud singing at times;
And when that singing is ended
I mimic, with arduous rhymès,
A song which I knew to be splendid,
And make of what I comprehended—
I singly—a thing so absurd
That rightly is reason offended.

What matter?—My rhymes are blurred
Because I wept when I heard
Proud singing whereof these rhymes
Iterate never a word;
And safely I treasure the times
Wherein is a song that climbs,
And my heart singly is stirred.

XIV

THE DARK COMPANION

" Nous sommes unités à cette fin "
—CHARLES GARNIER.

I AND MY SHADOW ARE SO MADE ONE
THAT WERE WE PARTED EACH LIFE WERE DONE.

Throughout the flight of the blithe bright day
Always he follows me, doggedly;
But I need not heed him,—because my way
Is flecked with sunlight,—and shrug to see
How fondly my Shadow follows me.

When dying day grows chill and stark,
And vigilant stars troop each to his place,
He rises,—being free in the dark,
He rises and grins,—being freed for a space,
He rises to talk with me face to face.

Then he tells me of much I am loth to hear,
For he whispers of all that we two have seen,
And loved, and squandered. *At forty year,*
My master, how wide is the gulf between
That which we are and what might have been!

And he whispers of dreams that the years degrade,
And of lust made lord over love's demesne,
And of chances wasted, and faith betrayed.
My master, how wide is the gulf between
That which we are and what might have been!

Even thus he whispers; and he and I
Sit thus, alone, till the night's defeat
Is signaled eastward, and chance thereby
Wins room for a morrow, fair and fleet,
That finds my Shadow beneath my feet.

I AND MY SHADOW ARE SO MADE ONE
THAT WERE WE PARTED EACH LIFE WERE DONE.

XV

SEA-SCAPES

I LIE and dream in the soft warm sand; and the thunder
    and surge and the baffled roar
Of the sea's relentless and vain endeavors are a pleasant
    lullaby, here on shore.

Since a little hillock screens yonder ageless tenacious
    battlings (which shatter, and pass
In foam and spume), I appraise, half-nodding, much
    sand and sky and gaunt nodding grass.

And I am content to lie and dream; and I am too drowsy
    to rise, and see
If it be worth breasting—that ocean yonder, which a
    little hillock hides from me.

VERTICORDIA

" A vous parle, compaings de galles "

I

BALLAD OF PLAGIARY

"Frères et maîtres, vous qui cultivez"
—PAUL VERVILLE.

HEY, my masters, lords and brothers, ye that till the
 fields of rhyme,
Are ye deaf ye will not hearken to the clamor of your
 time?

Still ye blot and change and polish—vary, heighten and
 transpose—
Old sonorous metres marching grandly to their tranquil
 close.

Ye have toiled and ye have fretted; ye attain perfected
 speech:
Ye have nothing new to utter and but platitudes to
 preach.

Still your rhymes are all of loving, as within the old
 days when
Love was lord of the ascendant in the horoscopes of men.

Still ye make of love the utmost end and scope of all
    your art,
And, more blind than he you write of, note not what a
    modest part
Loving now may claim in living, when we have scant
    time to spare,
Who are plundering the sea-depths, taking tribute of the
    air,—
Whilst the sun makes pictures for us; since to-day, for
    good or ill,
Earth and sky and sea are harnessed, and the lightnings
    work our will.

Hey, my masters, all these love-songs by dust-hidden
    mouths were sung
That ye mimic and re-echo with an artful-artless
    tongue,—
Sung by poets close to nature, free to touch her gar-
    ments' hem
Whom to-day ye know not truly; for ye only copy them.

Them ye copy, copy always, with your backs turned to
    the sun,
Caring not what man is doing, noting that which man
    has done.

We are talking over telephones, as Shakespeare could
    not talk;
We are riding out in motor-cars, where Homer had to
    walk;

And pictures Dante labored on of mediæval Hell
The nearest cinematograph paints quicker, and as well.

But ye copy, copy always;—and ye marvel when ye find
This new beauty, that new meaning,—while a model
    stands behind,
Waiting, young and fair as ever, till some singer turn
    and trace
Something of the deathless wonder of life lived in any
    place.

Hey, my masters, turn from piddling to the turmoil and
    the strife!
Cease from sonneting, my brothers; let us fashion songs
    from life.

THUS I WROTE ERE SYLVIA PASSED ME. . . . THEN DID I
    EPITOMIZE
ALL LIFE'S BEAUTY IN ONE POEM, AND MAKE HASTE TO
    EULOGIZE
QUITE THE FAIREST THING LIFE BOASTS OF, FOR I WROTE
    OF SYLVIA'S EYES.

II

THE AGELESS MAID

"Amors, qu'a escien m'a donat tal voler"
—Raimbaut de Vaqueiras.

Man's Love, that leads me day by day
Through many a screened and scented way,
Finds to assuage my thirst
No love that may the old love slay,
None sweeter than the first.

Fond heart of mine, that beats so fast
As this or that fair maid trips past,
Once, and with lesser stir,
We viewed the grace of love, at last,
And turned idolater.

Lad's Love it was, that in the spring
When all things woke to blossoming,
Was as a child that came
Laughing, and filled with wondering,
Nor knowing his own name.

And still—whatever years impend
To witness Time a fickle friend

And Youth a dwindling fire,—
I must adore till all years end
My first love, Heart's Desire.

I may not hear men speak of her
Unmoved, and vagrant pulses stir
To greet her passing-by,
And I, in all her worshipper,
Must serve her till I die.

For I remember: this is she
That reigns in one man's memory
Immune to age and fret,
And stays the maid I may nor see
Nor win to, nor forget.

III

FROM OVERSEA

"Domna, si no us vezon mei heulh"
—Raimbaut de Vaqueiras.

I

Félise, whose will, yet undiscerned, commands
My willing heart, stayest thou unmoved to see
How Love, forlorn and reft of empery,
Strains toward thy free heart with bleeding hands?
Now the last hour of day runs leaden sands
Hast thou indeed, Félise, no thought of me,
As all my thoughts take wing and throng to thee
Athwart the long leagues of dividing lands?

Félise, I am long sick with long delay,
Brain-wearied with long dreaming of thy grace,
Heart-hungered with long waiting in this place
Of days that are so long, whilst Love's own day,
Longed-for so long, draws on with leisured pace
To make thee mine, dear love so far away.

II

Félise, have pity!—cringing, at thy door
Entreats, with dolorous cry and clamoring,
That mendicant who quits thee nevermore:

124

Now winter chills the world, and no birds sing
In any woods, yet as in wanton spring
He follows thee ; and never will have done,
Though nakedly he die, from following
Whither thou leadest.

                    Canst thou look upon
His woes, and laugh to see a goddess' son
Of wide dominion, and in strategy
More strong than Jove, more wise than Solomon,
Inept to combat thy severity ?
Félise, have pity ! and let Love be one
Among the folk that bear thee company.

IV

COMPETITORS

—After Alessandro de Medici.

Heart o' My Heart, dost thou not hear
Tired waves, perturbed by the mystery
Of the voiding east where vext winds veer,
Lamenting and lisping?—*I, the Sea,*
Grapple and strain till I win to thee
I have loved so long, and may never depart
From that age-long siege till I win to thee,
Though I win as Enipëus, Heart o' My Heart.
     —The Sea's exordium
     Pleads thus, *cor cordium.*

Heart o' My Heart, dost thou not hear
A sighing of dying Winds?—crying to thee:—
We that were friendly with Guinevere,
And wafted Queen Helen oversea,
And served that lady of mystery
Balkis, a Sheban—caress and depart
Unwillingly, finding none fairer than thee
In those cold old venturings, Heart o' My Heart.
     —The Winds' exordium
     Sighs thus, *cor cordium.*

Heart o' My Heart, dost thou not hear
Love that strives—as the yearning Sea,
As the truant Winds,—for the sweet and austere
And sturdy and stainless heart of thee?—
Nay, without warning Love wins to thee
Suddenly some day, swift to impart
The secret of tears and the mystery
Of sorrow and heartbreak, Heart o' My Heart.
      —Without exordium
      Love takes, *cor cordium.*

All sighs and· tears are the Winds and the Sea,
And fit precursors—nay, portion and part
Of Love that is silent, and wins to thee
Silently some day, Heart o' My Heart.

THE STRIKING HOUR

"Comme un Croisé vaincu, qui longtemps languissait"
—NICOLAS DE CAEN.

I

As one imprisoned, that hath lain alone
And dreamed of sunlight where no vagrant gleam
Of sunlight pierces, being freed, must deem
This too but dreaming, and must dread the sun
Whose glory dazzles;—even as such-an-one
Am I, whose longing was but now supreme
For this high hour, and, now it strikes, esteem
I do but dream long dreamed-of goals are won.

Take heed! be still! lest haply God reprove.
We have climbed too high! Those note us overhead
Who know I am unworthy of your love;
And when yet-parted lips, sigh-visited,
End speech and wait, mine when I will to move,
Such joy awakens that I grow afraid.

II

Yet I have loved you in so many ways,—
With reverence always, and such purity
As often curbs that which is base in me;

And, though some folly oftentimes betrays
My purpose into naught, through all these days
Till this day I had striven silently
After some proof of my idolatry,
Some act not undeserving of your praise.

  To-day in flight from worldwide dissonance,
I storm your heart,—and claim not any fee
For any service rendered anywhere,
But as one comes to his inheritance
Demand admittance, knowing my love to be
No whit unworthy even to enter there.

III

  Catullus might have made of words that seek
With rippling sound, in soft recurrent ways,
The perfect song, or in remoter days
Theocritus have hymned you in glad Greek;
But I am not as they,—and dare not speak
Of you unworthily, and dare not praise
Perfection with imperfect roundelays,
And desecrate the prize I dare to seek.

  I do not woo you, then, by fashioning
Vext analogues 'twixt you and Guinevere;
Nor do I come with agile lips that bring
The sugared periods of a sonneteer,
And bring no more,—but just with lips that cling
To yours, in murmuring, *I love you, dear!*

VI

LIGHTS OF THE WORLD

—After CHARLES GARNIER.

SPEED forth, my song, the sun's ambassador,
Lest in the east night prove the conqueror,
And day be slain, and darkness triumph,—for
The sun is single, but her eyes are twain.

And now the sunlight and the night contest
A doubtful battle, and day bides at best
Doubtful, till Phyllis wake. It is attest
The sun is single.

     But her eyes are twain,—
And should the light of all the world delay,
And darkness prove victorious? Is it day
Now that the sun alone is risen?

        Nay,
The sun is single, but her eyes are twain,—
Twain firmaments that mock with heavenlier hue
The heavens' less lordly and less gracious blue,
And lit with sunlier sunlight through and through.

The sun is single, but her eyes are twain,
And of fair things this side of Paradise
Fairest, of goodly things most goodly.

                                    Rise!
And succor the benighted world that cries,
The sun is single, but her eyes are twain!

VII

"—OF ANISE AND CUMMIN ALSO"

—After NICOLAS DE CAEN.

IT IS in vain I mirror forth the praise
In pondered virelais
Of her that is the lady of my love;
Far-sought and curious phrases fail to tell
The tender miracle
Of her white body and the grace thereof.

Thus many and many an artful-artless strain
Is fashioned all in vain:
Sound proves unsound; and even her name, that is
To me more glorious than the glow of fire
Or dawn or love's desire
Or opals interlinked with turquoises,
Mocks utterance.

So, lacking skill to praise
That perfect bodily beauty which is hers,
Even as those worshippers
Who bore rude offerings of honey and maize,
Their all, into the gold-paved ministers
Of Aphroditê, I have given her these
My faltering melodies,
That are Love's lean and ragged messengers.

132

VIII

"SWEET ADELAIS"

—After Raimbaut de Vaqueiras.

Had you lived when earth was new
What had bards of old to do
Save to sing in praise of you?

Had you lived in ancient days,
Adelais, sweet Adelais,
You had all the ancients' praise,—
You whose beauty would have won
Canticles of Solomon,
Had the sage Judean king
Gazed upon this goodliest thing
Earth of Heaven's grace hath got.

Had you gladdened Greece, were not
All the nymphs of Greece forgot?

Had you trod Sicilian ways,
Adelais, sweet Adelais,
You had pilfered all their praise:
Bion and Theocritus
Had transmitted unto us
Honeyed harmonies to tell

133

Of your beauty's miracle,
Delicate, desirable,
And their singing skill were bent
You-ward tenderly,—content,
While the world slipped by, to gaze
On the grace of you, and praise
Sweet Adelais.

Had you lived in Roman times
No Catullus in his rhymes
Had lamented Lesbia's sparrow:
He had praised your forehead, narrow
As the newly-crescent moon,
White as apple-trees in June;
He had made some amorous tune
Of the laughing light Erôs
Snared as Psychê-ward he goes
By your beauty,—by your slim,
White, perfect beauty.

After him
Horace, finding in your eyes
Horace limned in lustrous wise,
Would have made you melodies
Fittingly to hymn your praise,
Sweet Adelais.

Had your father's household been
Guelfic-born or Ghibelline,
Beatricê were unknown
On her star-encompassed throne.

For, had Dante viewed your grace,
Adelais, sweet Adelais,
You had reigned in Bicê's place,—
Had, for candles, Hyades,
Rastaben, and Betelguese,—
And had heard Zachariel
Chant of you, and, chanting, tell
All the grace of you, and praise
Sweet Adelais.

Had you lived when earth was new
What had bards of old to do
Save to sing in praise of you?

They had sung of you always,
Adelais, sweet Adelais,
As worthiest of all men's praise;
Nor had undying melodies
Wailed soft as love may sing of these
Dream-hallowed names,—of Héloïse,
Ysoude, Salomê, Semelê,
Morgaine, Lucrece, Antiopê,
Brunhilda, Helen, Mélusine,
Penelopê, and Magdalene:
—But you alone had all men's praise,
Sweet Adelais.

IX

LOVE'S LOVERS

—After Raimbaut de Vaqueiras.

*Nor had undying melodies
Wailed soft as love may sing of these
That are love's martyrs,—Héloïse,
Brunhilda, Helen, Mélusine,
Antiopê, and Magdalene,—
Ysoude, Salomê, Semelê,
Lucretia, and Penelopê.*

What of these ladies that have been
Exalted by stern songs wherein
Beats strong the valorous heart of Love
And all the power and pride thereof—
Unto what haven are they sped?

Because they are not wholly dead:
The Land of Matters Unforgot
They walk at will, where time is not
And death has no dominion,—
And there they never view the sun,
But through a vague and amiable
Hushed twilight pass, and, passing, tell
Their tale of ancient miseries,
And neither laugh nor weep.

     To these,
Whose lives were troubled harmonies
Whereby the heart of Love yet is
Enamored, Love at last accords
An end of love. To these, the Lords
Of Life and Death, that kindled lust,
And wrath, and joy frail as blown dust,
And faith like flame that braves the wind;
And kindled for each sin they sinned
Fame, and for every misery fame
Set as a flaring star to flame
And blaze and glow above the seas
Where light love founders: have granted peace
Unvexed by heart-beats.—Thus they pass,
Desiring naught of life that was
Exhausted of all things long ago,—
With void eyes, emptied of woe,
Emptied of joy, pass hand-in-hand,
Being shadows in a shadow land.

  The story of their love is writ
In song; the valiant sound of it
Endures unaltered evermore:
But we, that love as heretofore
These loved, must perish, as they, and be
Forgotten by all men utterly.

  I cry *Content!* Our names will die.
I cry *Content!* and cheerily,
Félise.

Our love-songs are unsung,
Yet we have loved. We have been young
In April and in unison . . .
Oblivious of oblivion,
And heedless of each after-year,
How well we lived our verses, dear!

X

TOUCHING UBIQUITY

" Voulant faire un cadeau digne de la plus belle"
—CHARLES GARNIER.

I

THE gods in honor of my Sylvia's worth
Bore gifts to her:—and Jove, Olympus' lord,
Co-rule of Earth and Heaven did accord,
And Hermes brought that lyre he framed at birth,
And Venus her famed girdle (to engirth
A fairer beauty now), and Mars his sword,
And wrinkled Plutus half the secret hoard
And immemorial treasure of mid-earth;—

And while the careful gods were pondering
Which of these goodly gifts the goodliest was,
Young Cupid came among them carolling
And proffered unto her a looking-glass,
Wherein she gazed and saw the goodliest thing
That Earth had borne, and Heaven might not surpass.

II

Whereafter he invaded Hell, and drove
Before him all the hosts of Erebus,

Till he had conquered; and grim Cerberus
Sang madrigals, the Furies rhymed of love,
Old Charon sighed, and sonnets rang above
The gloomy Styx; and even as Tantalus
Was Prosperine discrowned in Tartarus,
And Cupid regnant in the place thereof.

Thus Love is monarch throughout Hell to-day;
In Heaven we know his power was always great;
And Earth acclaimed Love's mastery straightway
When Sylvia came to gladden Earth's estate:—
Thus Hell and Heaven and Earth his rule obey,
And Sylvia's heart alone is obdurate.

XI

FANCIES IN FILIGREE

—Strambotti of A<small>LESSANDRO</small> <small>DE</small> M<small>EDICI</small>.

XXIV

"Guarda negli occhi la nostra regina"

M<small>Y</small> Lady's Eyes Remembrance bring
Of lyttel Waves whose Wavering
Beneathe ye roving Summer Breeze
Makes scintillant hushed Summer Seas
Whenas ye Sun is vanishing.

They gladden me, as when in Spring
We sing & knowe not why we sing.
In sooth, there be noe Eyes like these
My Lady's Eyes.

Whenas their Glance is threatening
They frighten Cupid, & that King
From Florimel a-quaking flees;
But when they soften, on hys Knees
Love falls before them worshipping
My Lady's Eyes.

XLI

"Rime d'amore usar dolci e leggiadre"

Ye little Rhyme I swore last Night
To lay before ye Eyes so bright
I have long loved—& loved too wéll!—
So now ye Muses to compell,
& shapely Phrases to indite.

Which shall it be?—Ye Villanelle,
Ode, Triolet, Rondeau, Rondel,
Ballade, or Sonnet?—Each is hight
        Ye littel Rhyme.

Yet none will aide my hapless Plight:
All little Rhymes are short & slight,
& of ye Charmes of Florimel
An Epick's Length alone can tell,—
So that of her I may not write
        Ye lyttel Rhyme.

XII

IT IS ENOUGH

—After Nicolas de Caen.

Love me or love me not, it is enough
That I have loved you, seeing my whole life is
Uplifted and made glad by the glory of Love,—
My life that was a scroll bescrawled and blurred
With tavern-catches, which that pity of his
Erased, and wrote instead one lonely word,
    Yolande!

I have accorded you incessant praise
And song and service, dear, because of this;
And always I have dreamed incessantly
Who always dreamed,—*When in oncoming days
This man or that shall love you, and at last
This man or that shall win you, it must be
That, loving him, you will have pity on me
When happiness engenders memory
And long thoughts nor unkindly of the past,*
    Yolande!

Of this I know not surely,—who am sure
That I shall always love you while I live,
And that, when I am dead, with naught to give

Of song or service, Love will yet endure,
And yet retain his last prerogative,
When I lie still, and sleep out centuries
With dreams of you and the exceeding love
I bore you, and am glad dreaming thereof,
And give God thanks for all, and so find peace,
        Yolande!

XIII

AN ARCADIAN APOLOGIZES

—After CHARLES GARNIER.

I PRAY you do not marvel, dear, that I,
Whenever with fond hardihood I try
To rhyme your praises, fail ingloriously.

And marvel not that I in happier wise
Have hymned Félise and lauded Sylvia's eyes,
And now may offer you no melodies.

We poets are so made that when we be
Unscathed by love none wooes so well as we,
But, wounded once, we worship silently.

XIV

ARCADIANS CONFER IN EXILE

—After CHARLES GARNIER.

I

So long ago it was! Nay, is it true
In verity we passed a month or so
In Arcady when life and love were new
    So long ago?

The tide of time's indomitable flow,
Augmenting, rears a drearier realm, whereto
We twain are exiled. Yet . . . I do not know . . .
Now that a woman calls, whose eyes are blue,
Whose speech is gracious—strangely sweet and low
She calls, and smiles as STELLA used to do
    So long ago.

II

I am not fit to follow; yet I pray
Some mighty task be set me, to commit
In her dear name, for trifles to essay
    I am not fit.

Nay, I, unstable and bereft of wit—
Even I!—return to my old love to-day,
Whose bounty is so fond and infinite
That I am heartened, and made strong, and may
Not ever falter in deserving it,
If but for dread lest of such grace men say
      I am not fit.

III

Time has changed naught in us; for now the din
And darkness of tempestuous years, that wrought
So vainly, lift; and it is lightly seen
      Time has changed naught.

Such knowledge of those brawling years I bought:
The thing which shall be is that which has been,
When heaven again surprises us, unsought,
And life returns full circle; and we win
Again to realms which with how little thought
We ceded, and find loyalty wherein
      Time has changed naught.

IV

Sweetheart, I wait; now, as in time gone by,
Your suppliant, half-frightened, half-elate,
Outside the trellised doors of Arcady,
      Sweetheart, I wait.

Again I glimpse its meadows—through a grate,
Alas!—and streams and groves and cloudless sky;
And cry to you to be compassionate,—
Yea, as of old to STELLA, now I cry
To you that once were STELLA; and my fate
Attends your piloting, for whose reply,
        Sweetheart, I wait.

XV

THE EAVESDROPPERS

—After ALPHONSE MOREAU.

THE heart of the twilight is troubled; and there
Where the stubbled fields bathe in colorless air,
And show as the chin of a giant unshorn,
Dog-weary, and dreaming of days unborn,
The east is perturbed; and night kindles to morn.

Wide world, that wakes to each miracle
Each dawn engenders, thou wilt not tell,
If mother of me indeed thou art,
How gladly and furtively I depart
Master and lord of Phyllida's heart.

Hah, Lady Moon, so we meet again!
I remember. Who silvered the window-pane,
Climbed over heaped faggots with noiseless tread,
Turned velvet the cobwebs that gleamed overhead,
Stealthily, hearkening to all we said?

Eavesdropper, keep my secret well!
Remember the tales that old poets tell

Of the Latmian hills, and a cave thereon
Whereinto passed when each day was done—
Eavesdropper!—not only Endymion.

  Ye will not tell of it. Nor will he,
The owl that hoots now in yonder tree,
And flutters his wings, with a watchful eye
Bent through the boughs at a passer-by
Who laughs, in the dawn . . . and he wonders why.

APATURIA

"Ainsi m'ont amours abusé"

I

GRAY DAYS

—After Nicolas de Caen.

I can find no meaning in life,
That have weighed the world,—and it was
Abundant with folly, and rife
With sorrows brittle as glass,
And with joys that flicker and pass
Like dreams through a fevered head;
And as the dripping of rain
In gardens naked and dead
Is the obdurate thin refrain
Of our youth which is presently dead.

And Chloris, whom last I loved,
Looks ever with loathing on me,
As one she hath seen disproved
And stained with such smirches as be
Not ever cleansed utterly;
And is loth to remember the days
When Destiny fixed her name
As the theme and the goal of my praise;
And my love engenders shame,
And I stain what I strive for and praise.

153

Chloris, most perfect of all,
Just to have known you is well!
And it heartens me now to recall
That just to have known you is well,
And naught else is desirable
Save only to do as you willed
And to love you my whole life long;—
But this heart in me is filled
With hunger cruel and strong,
And with hunger unfulfilled.

Fond heart, though thy hunger be
As a flame that wanders unstilled,
There is none more perfect than she!

II

A WOOD-PIECE: TO THE WHIR OF FALLING
LEAVES

Yes, you will soon forget. Leaf-shadowed ways
Are disenchanted now; the kindly haze
Of love-light lifts from too-long loitering;
A kiss is now at most two lips that cling;
And mirth is dead now; and desire decays.

Even now Love flutters restive wings, and stays
Impatient of restraint, what while I praise
Love's old lost favor, past replevining,—
              But you will soon forget.

Yes, you will soon forget: and naught betrays
That any heart save mine even now inveighs
In futile rage because nor youth nor spring
Can stay or solace light love's vanishing.
I shall remember, dear, through all my days,
              But you will soon forget.

III

LOVE GOES INTO WINTER QUARTERS
—After Antoine Riczi.

(The Scene a dale, somewhere in Arcady,
But filled with snow and sleet, made horrible
By many tramplings; there anon must be
A Crier, robed in black and with a bell;
To whom a Poet, peering curiously.)

"What art thou calling, O sombre Crier,—
Who plays the fugitive? who is beguiled?
Is it a theft or a house to hire,
A sheriff's sale or a stolen child?"

For none of these do I play the crier, .
And toll a reward where the winds are wild,
And I strive knee-deep in the sleet and the mire
In quest of a kingdom undefiled.

"Reward, quoth he!—and how darest thou prattle
Of guerdon-giving, that goest in black,
Sans cap and sandals, where bleak winds battle
Which first may strip the rags from thy back?"

Of no compulsion save my own pleasure's
I wear this black—for a mourning sign,—
Till Yesterday waken, and yield the treasures
And gold-wrought garments which once were mine.

"Faith, only a madman dreams to muster
The bygone hours, bid them live again . . .
Though Crœsus wheedle or Charlemagne bluster,
Time heeds not at all, and they strive in vain."

Nay, Time forgets them; for these—unlanded,
Unkinged, uncarnate, and cold,—lie hid
Where Time comes never, to be commanded;—
Time cannot hear through the coffin's lid.

"So it matters naught with what pomp they wended,
What queens they wed, and what realms they won!
These things were goodly; these things are ended;
And naught sleeps sounder than joy fordone."

Cry Absit omen! the sermon is stupid—
Hey, even of sermons I grow afraid,
Who am no madman, but outlawed CUPID,
With never a place to lay my head.

But Yesterday! for Yesterday!
I cry a reward for a Yesterday
Now lost or stolen or gone astray,
With all the laughter of Yesterday!

(FOR WE HAVE MADE AN END OF AMOROUS PLAYING,
AND SHALLOW-HEARTED LOVE IS TURNED ASTRAY,
WITH CHILDISH SORROWING AND WEAK-VOICED PRAYING
FOR YESTERDAY.)

IV

FLOTSAM

WE did not share the same inheritance,—
I and this woman, five years older than I,
Yet daughter of a later century,—
Who is therefore only wearied by that dance
Which has set my blood a-leaping.

                         It is queer
To note how kind her face grows, listening
To my wild talk, and plainly pitying
My callow youth, and seeing in me a dear
Amusing boy,—yet somewhat old to be
Still reading *Alice through the Looking-Glass*
And *Water Babies*. . . .

                    With light talk we pass.

And I that have lived long in Arcady—
I that have kept so many a foolish tryst,
And written drivelling rhymes—feel stirring in me
Droll pity for this woman who pities me,
And whose weak mouth so many men have kissed.

V

HEIRS UNAPPARENT

How very heartily I hate
The man that will love you,
Some day, somewhere, and more than I,
And with a love more true;—
Whom for that reason you will love
As you may not love me,—
Though I might hold your heart, I think,
Held I one heart in fee.

My dear, too many ghosts arise
Between us when I woo,
One mocking me with softer lips,
And one with eyes more blue,
And one with hands more fine than yours,
And one with lovelier hair,
Proclaiming:—*She is fair enough,
But then . . . I too was fair.*

What of thy heart thou gavest me
("And me!"—"And me!")—*is thine
No more to give again. That part
Is mine.*—("And mine!"—"And mine!")

And he that plays with love too long
Gets love of many-an-one,
But is denied Love's crowning grace,
And can give love to none.

Since these be truthful ghosts, I shrug
And woo you without tears
Or too much laughter, till with time
A properer Prince appears,
Whom very heartily I hate,—
The man that will love you,
Some day, somewhere, and more than I,
And with a love more true.

VI

LIGHT COINAGE

—"MERCURIENS": PAUL VERVILLE.

XX

"C'est une comédie, qui termine aujourd'huy"

THAT comedy we end, content to please
Its players merely, was a comedy
Wherein Love had no part. It may not be
Enrolled among Love's mighty memories,
And men unborn will read of Héloïse,
And Ruth, and Rosamond, and Semelê,
When none remembers your name's melody
Or rhymes your name enregistered with these.

And will my name wake moods as amorous
As that of Abélard or Lancelot
Arouses? be recalled when Pyramus
And Tristram are unrhymed of and forgot?—
Time's laughter answers, who accords to us
More gracious fields, wherein we harvest—what?

162

XXIII

" Voicy! un autre chante!—Il n'est pas interdit"

A singer, eh? . . . Well, well! but when he sings
Take jealous heed lest idiosyncrasies
Entinge and taint too deep his melodies;
See that his lute has no discordant strings
To harrow us; and let his vaporings
Be all of virtue and its victories,
And of man's best and noblest qualities,
And scenery, and flowers, and similar things.

Thus bid our paymasters, whose mutterings
Some few deride, and blithely link their rhymes
At random; and, as ever, on frail wings
Of wine-stained paper scribbled with such rhymes
Men mount to heaven, and loud laughter springs
From hell's midpit, whose fuel is such rhymes.

VII

THE SUN'S HIGHWAY

—After Antoine Riczi.

Though long be the way to the Limit of Lands,
And through leagues and leagues of treacherous sands,
And miles of marsh and mire,
I must win, if at all, to the rim of the west
Ere I enter that region the sun loves best,
Yet therein is my heart's desire.

And lately I learned of a pleasanter way
Which two of us travel on every day;
Oh, whatever a staid world deems,
We only are free of that road, I wot,—
The sun in his flamy chariot,
And I in my car of dreams.

Whereby we win to a land of ease
In whose stately beautiful palaces
Wracked lives are lived anew,—
For the sun and I go on pilgrimage
To the lovelier land of a younger age,
Where what might have been is true.

I do not know on what lordly quest
The sun fares sturdily into the west,
But I know that he goes with joy,
And espies, perhaps, past the mountained rim
Repentant Daphnê awaiting him,
Or Creusa no longer coy.

There, too, she waits whom alone I love;
And a chill light heart that I could not move
And bright eyes which would not see
My heart's hard hunger, no more the same,
Enkindle and nourish love's lovely flame,
And its beacon burns for me.

Well! I must win to her; I must kneel—
Kneel at her naked feet—and feel
Soft hands that caress my hair
Silently—oh, in such tender wise
That I shall not hasten to raise tired eyes
To a face however fair.

Fair face unstained by the grave's eclipse!
Fair face that lifts now to no man's lips
And troubles no man's sleep!
The woman that wore you has children now . . .
But that is nothing; I keep my vow,
And I have a tryst to keep.

And so in a world whose tumults seem
Intriguing shadows I tread, and dream
Of a maiden who dreams of me:
For the tryst is set; be it late, be it soon,
Or east of the sun or west of the moon,
I shall win to you, Dorothy.

VIII

THE OLDEST DITTY

—After Nicolas de Caen.

And so farewell;—for now assuredly
Did the long pulse of the profoundest sea,
So deep it knows not light nor any heat,
Vex now some seaweed thick about my feet
Which there had nodded through a century,
All faith in you were not more dead in me,—
     And so farewell!

And so, *Farewell!* I cry,—that may not see
Love quicken in the eyes of Dorothy
Ever again, nor evermore repeat
Mad rhymes to her, nor ever bend to meet
Her lips this side of all eternity;—
Love hath nowhere enfixed pre-potency,
    And so farewell!

IX

TO THE SAME AIR AS THE PRECEDING

And so farewell (as my rondeau wails
In obsolete accents and absolute truth),
For all is over, and nothing avails
To capture the rapture of last year's youth.

All is quite over. Touch hands. Good-bye.
For you the future is nowise dim;
For me there are other women, and I
Must forget you now, since that is your whim.

And we will laugh in the after-times
At two young people we knew, no doubt,
Who scribbled each other such woeful rhymes
And played a comical tragedy out.

We shall not die of it. We shall be
Contented and healed of the passing smart;
And yet if you had not tired of me,
Life while life lasted were yours, sweetheart.

X

GRAVE GALLANTRY

—After Charles Garnier.

I

My rival Death is fashioned amorously;—
No caliph boasts more comely wives than he,
For whom crowned Cleopatra reft the snare
Of careful-eyed Octavius, and—less fair
Than she, but lovely still—Leucothoë,
And Atalanta, and Antigonê,
Loosed virgin zones. . . . What need hadst thou to be
Desirous then of this girl's lips and hair,
    My rival Death?

What need hadst thou likewise of Dorothy!
What need of that which was all life to me!
What need, lascivious Death, that she forswear
Fond oaths to me—fond oaths made otherwhere—
In thy lank arms, and leave me friends with thee,
    My rival, Death!

II

Had she divined how many virelais
Have feebly parodied some piercing phase
Of love for her whom love lacked might to claim—
How many rhymes have marshalled frail and lame,
Yet fervent-hearted, to avouch her praise,—
Such pity had been mine as well repays
Drear years of waiting.—Ey, in kindlier days
Compassion might have worn some kinglier name
　　　Had she divined.

Now that may never be; divergent ways
Allured; and all is ended; and naught betrays
Dead cheeks to kindle, now, with livelier flame
For aught I utter. . . . Yet it were no shame
To dream a little on her softening gaze
　　　Had she divined.

III

That she is dead breeds no uncouth despair,
However,—as death bred when men would bear
A glove upon their helms, and slay or sing
In honor of its giver, hazarding
Life and life's aims because a girl was fair . . .
Grotesque their liege-lord seems when we compare
That Cupidling who spurs me to declare
Sedate regret, in rhythmic sorrowing
　　　That she is dead.

Nay, he is much the punier of the pair,—
My little lord, who dreads lest critics stare
Too pointedly,—a flimsy fainéant king;—
Yet hearts may crack without crude posturing.
This girl is dead; and I confess I care
    That she is dead.

XI

BY-WORDS

—After Alphonse Moreau.

Not even now in all things may there be
An end of folly; nor, as mutineers
Against love's lunacy, that now appears
Of no more weight or worth or urgency
Than last night's dreams,—not wholly yet may we
Become in all things like all our compeers,
That are armored by interminable years
And keep no vestige of insanity.

What yet remains, now we drift far apart,
With seas between, and each of us forgets
The happenings of all our happy days?—
Your by-words, heard on other lips, to raise
Love's pitiable phantom in my heart,
And waken mirthful memories and regrets.

XII

ANOTHER LABORER WEIGHS HIS HIRE

"Amors, tant vos ai servit"
—Raimbaut de Vaqueiras.

Lord, I have worshipped thee ever,—
Through all these years
I have served thee, forsaking never
Light Love that veers
As a child between laughter and tears.
Hast thou no more to afford,—
Naught save laughter and tears,—
Love, my lord?

I have borne thy heaviest burden,
Nor served thee amiss:
When thou hast given a guerdon,
Lo, it was this—
A sigh, a shudder, a kiss.
Hast thou no more to accord?
I would have more than this,
Love, my lord.

I am wearied of love that is pastime
And gifts that it brings;
I entreat of thee, lord, at this last time

Ineffable things.
Nay, have proud long-dead kings
Stricken no subtler chord,
Whereof the memory clings,
Love, my lord?

But for a little we live;
Show me thine innermost hoard!
Hast thou no more to give,
Love, my lord?

XIII

RETRACTIONS

—After Théodore Passerat.

YOU ASK A SONNET?—WELL, IT IS YOUR RIGHT.
I GRANT IT, LAUGH, SHRUG, SET ABOUT THE TASK,
AND MAKE A SEQUENCE, SINCE IT IS MY RIGHT
NO MORE TO GIVE YOU ONLY WHAT YOU ASK.

1

ALTHOUGH as yet my cure be incomplete,
Yet love of you, time-lulled and vigorless,
Engenders now no more unhappiness,
Not even discontent. And now we meet
Unmoved—half-waggish,—and my pulses beat
Quite calmly as I wonder now, *Is he
As proud as I was? and—as once to me—
To him is her love lovely and very sweet?*

Nor do I grudge him any joy of his
Who follows on a road that I have trod,
And sues for love where I was wont to sue;
I am contented by remembrances,
And know that neither Fate nor Time, nor God,
Robs me of that first mastery of you.

175

2

I am contented by remembrances,—
Dreams of dead passions, wraiths of vanished times,
Fragments of vows, and by-ends of old rhymes,—
Flotsam and jetsam tumbling in the seas
Whereon, long since, put forth our argosies
Which, launched for traffic in the Isles of Love,
Lie foundered somewhere in some firth thereof,
Encradled by eternal silences.

Thus, having come to naked bankruptcy,
Let us part friends, as thrifty tradesmen do
When common ventures fail; for it may be
These battered oaths and rhymes may yet ring true
To some fair woman's hearing, so that she
Will listen and think of love, and I of you.

3

You have chosen the love "that lives sans murmurings,
Sans passion," and incuriously endures
The gradual lapse of time. You have chosen as yours
A level life of little happenings;
And through the long autumnal evenings
Lord Love, no doubt, is of the company,
And hugs your ingleside contentedly,
Smiles at old griefs, and rustles needless wings.

And yet I think that sometimes memories
Of divers trysts, of blood that urged like wine

On moonlit nights, and of that first long kiss
Whereby your lips were first made one with mine,
Awake and trouble you, and loving is
Once more important and perhaps divine.

4

You have chosen; and I cry content thereto,
And cry your pardon also, and am reproved
In that I took you for a woman I loved
Odd centuries ago, and would undo
That curious error. Nay, your eyes are blue,
Your speech is gracious, but you are not she;
And I am older,—and changed how utterly!—
I am no longer I, you are not you.

Time, destined as we thought but to befriend
And guerdon love like ours, finds you beset
With joys and griefs I neither share nor mend
Who am a stranger; and we two are met
Nor wholly glad nor sorry, and the end
Of too much laughter is a faint regret.

5

It is in many ways made plain to us
That love must grow like any common thing,
Root, bud, and leaf, ere ripe for garnering
The mellow fruitage front us; even thus
Must Helena encounter Thesëus
Ere Paris come, and every century

Spawn divers queens who die with Antony
But live a great while first with Julius.

Thus I have spoken the prologue of a play
Wherein I have no part, and laugh, and sit
Contented in the wings, whilst you portray
An amorous maid with gestures that befit
This lovely rôle,—as who knows better, pray,
Than I that helped you in rehearsing it?

6

With Love I garnered mirth, and dreams, and shame;
And half his playmate, half his worshipper,
I flouted him, and yet might not demur
To do his bidding, or in aught diffame
Love's tutorage,—not even when you came,
And at the portal of Love's golden house
We hazarded stray kisses, sighs and vows,
And lightly staked them in a hackneyed game.

And now the game is ended, dear; and we
May not re-enter that august domain
Which we, encoasting, lost eternally;
And now, although beloved by many men,
You may love no man as you have loved me,
Who have loved you as I may not love again.

7

Unto how many futures I was heir
In those old talks, which fixed what must be done

When we at last should rule (in Babylon
Perhaps, or in Caer-Is, or Kennaquahair),
And must do this or that, and bravely share
Fantastic fates, whose frolic freakishness
Seems how less quaint than this is,—to confess
That I have lost you, and do not greatly care!

Well! had we never cared, in all that fleet
Sweet time which passed so swiftly and is gone—
And gone eternally!—yet it was sweet
To play at loving, for all that every groan,
And gainless grieving, was in counterfeit
And parody of love, ungained, unknown.

8

And so we played at loving. So we played
With love as venturous children in the sea
Wade ankle-deep, and laugh, and wistfully
Peer at the world's far rim, being half-afraid,
Half-wistful. So we laughed, and we obeyed
That changeless law which sways the cosmic plan,
And ever draws the maid unto the man,
And ever draws the man unto the maid.

The sea hides deep our fragile argosy,
And idle doubts quest fruitlessly above
Those shattered hulks, too frail to brave the sea,
Too frail to brave the wrath and mirth thereof:
I had not heart to love you heartily,
You were too shrewd to be befooled by love.

9

Time was I coveted the woes they rued
Whose love commemorates them—I that meant
To get like grace of love then!—and intent
To win, as they had done, love's plenitude,
Rapture and havoc, vauntingly I sued
That love like theirs might make a toy of me,
At will caressed, at will (if publicly)
Demolished, as Love found or found not good.

To-day I am no longer overbrave.
I have a fever—I that always knew
This hour was certain!—and am too weak to rave,
Too tired to seek (as later I must do)
Tried remedies—time, manhood and the grave,—
To drug, abate and banish love of you.

10

Time was I loved you. . . . And indeed I came
To love you so time hardly washes out
The scars of an old moment which, as flame
Leaps toward chaff, bereft me even of doubt:
And then indeed I knew you had deceived me—
You, even you!—and counterfeiting truth
So cunningly that you and I believed me,
I cried, *I will forget!* . . . This was in youth.

Now, being older and less over-nice,
I estimate these follies, breed of them
My little books,—shift, polish and re-price
The jewels of a battered diadem,—
And cry, *What hope of heaven for those who sell
What I am vending? and what need of hell?*

11

We are as time moulds us, lacking wherewithal
To shape out nobler fortunes or contend
Against all-patient Fates, who may not mend
The allotted pattern of things temporal,
Or alter it a thread's-width, or let fall
A single stitch thereof, until at last
The web and its drear weavers be overcast,
And predetermined darkness swallow all.

They have ordained for us a time to sing,
A time to love, a time wherein to tire
Of all spent songs and kisses; carolling
Such elegies as buried dreams require,
Love now departs, and leaves us shivering
Beside the embers of a burned-out fire.

12

Cry *Kismet!* and take heart. Erôs is gone,
Nor may we follow to that loftier air
Olympians breathe. Take heart, and enter where
A lighter love-lord takes a heatless sun,

Oblivious of tangled webs ill-spun
By ancient wearied weavers, for it may be
His guidance leads to lovers of such as we
And hearts so credulous as to be won.

Cry *Kismet!* Put away vain memories
Of all old sorrows and of all old joys,
And learn that life is never quite amiss
So long as unreflective girls and boys
Remember that young lips were meant to kiss,
And hold that laughter is a seemly noise.

13

So, let us laugh . . . How quaint that even I
Was once a fool such as each fool bemocks,
Burlesques and shames! how droll a paradox
It is that we meet calmly! nor deny
That I in an old time dared to be I,
And you in that same season dared be you,
When commonly we wooed (as others do,
And we do not, now) dreams which do not die,—

But take new life, with new idolaters,
Among our juniors; and in naught are kin
To our time-tempered blood which, drowsing, stirs
A little, recollecting with what din
And ardor we assailed stark barriers
Proved obdurate ere we were locked therein.

14

So, let us laugh,—lest vain rememberings
Breed, as of old, some rude bucolic cry
Of awkward anguishes, of dreams that die
Without decorum, of Love lacking wings
Yet striving you-ward in his flounderings
Eternally,—as now, even when I lie
As I lie now, who know that you and I
Exist and heed not lesser happenings.

I was. I am. I will be. Eh, no doubt
For some sufficient cause, I drift, defer,
Equivocate, dream, hazard, grow more stout,
Age, am no longer Love's idolater,—
And yet I could and would not live without
Your faith that heartens and your doubts which spur.

15

Nightly I mark and praise, or great or small,
Such stars as proudly struggle one by one
To heaven's highest place, as Procyon,
Antarês, Naös, Tejat and Nibal
Attain supremacy, and proudly fall,
Still glorious, and glitter, and are gone
So very soon;—whilst steadfast and alone
Polaris gleams, and is not changed at all.

Daily I find some gallant dream that ranges
The heights of heaven ; and as others do,
I serve my dream until my dream estranges
Its errant bondage, and I note anew
That nothing dims, nor shakes, nor mars, nor changes,
Fond faith in you and in my love of you.

AND THEREFORE PRAISE I EVEN THE MOST HIGH
LORD CHANCE,—THAT, BEING OF KIN WITH SETEBOS,
IN ORDERING LIFE'S LABOR, STRIFE AND LOSS,
ORDAINED THAT YOU BE YOU, AND I BE I.

XIV

GARDEN-SONG

"Adieu, nous n'irons plus aux champs"
—Charles Garnier.

Farewell to Fields and Butterflies
And levities of Yester-year!
For we espy, and hold more dear,
The Wicket of our Destinies.

Whereby we enter, once for all,
A Garden which such Fruit doth yield
As, tasted once, no more Afield
We fare where Youth holds carnival.

Farewell, fair Fields, none found amiss
When laughter was a frequent noise
And golden-hearted girls and boys
Appraised the mouth they meant to kiss.

Farewell, farewell! but for a space
We, being young, Afield might stray,
That in our Garden nod and say,
Afield is no unpleasant place.

XV

AT PARTING

Thus then I end my calendar
Of ancient loves more light than air;—
And now Lad's Love, that led afar
In April fields that were so fair,
Is fled, and I no longer share
Sedate unutterable days
With Heart's Desire, nor ever praise
Félise, or mirror forth the lures
Of Stella's eyes nor Sylvia's,
Yet love for each loved lass endures.

Chloris is wedded, and Ettarre
Forgets; Yolande loves otherwhere,
And worms long since made bold to mar
The lips of Dorothy and fare
Mid Florimel's bright ruined hair;
And Time obscures that roseate haze
Which glorified hushed woodland ways
When Phyllis came. as Time obscures
That faith which once was Phyllida's,—
Yet love for each loved lass endures.

That boy is dead as Schariar,
Tiglath-pileser, or Clotaire,
Who once of love got many a scar.
And his loved lasses past compare?—
None is alive now anywhere.
Each is transmuted nowadays
Into a stranger, and displays
No whit of love's investitures.
I let these women go their ways,
Yet love for each loved lass endures.

Heart o' My Heart, thine be the praise
If aught of good in me betrays
Thy tutelage—whose love matures
Unmarred in these more wistful days,—
Yet love for each loved lass endures.

EXPLICIT